Love, Lust & A Millionaire

Sandi Lynn

Sandi Lynn

Love, Lust & A Millionaire

Copyright © 2015 Sandi Lynn

Cover Design by Cassy Roop @Pink Ink Designs

Photography by Sara Eirew @Sarah Eirew Photography

Models: Manuel Magnan & Joanna Skrzypczak Ardila

Editing by B.Z. Hercules

Table of Contents

BOOKS BY SANDI LYNN

The Forever Series:

Forever Black, Forever You, Forever Us, Being Julia

A Forever Christmas, Collin

A Millionaire's Love Series:

Lie Next To Me, When I Lie With You

Love Series:

Love In Between, The Upside of Love

Stand Alones:

His Proposed Deal

A Love Called Simon

She Writes Love

Then You Happened

Remembering You (A Novella)

Chapter 1

"Delilah, wake up! You're going to be late for work again."

I opened my eyes. Jenny, my roommate, was staring down at me. "Remember what Frank said? He said he'd fire you if you were late again!"

"Shit." I grabbed my phone from the coffee table. It was eight thirty. *Double shit.* "Why didn't you wake me earlier?" I jumped up from the couch.

"I did and you said you were getting up. I just got back from my run."

I ran into the bathroom, dabbed some toothpaste on my toothbrush, and vigorously brushed my teeth as I ran to my bedroom, picking up yesterday's jeans off the floor, throwing them on, and grabbing the red t-shirt that displayed "Frank's Diner" across my chest. After spitting in the sink and rinsing my mouth, I ran a brush through my long, brown hair and threw it up in a ponytail. Tossing my makeup in my purse, I grabbed it and flew out the door. I had exactly ten minutes to get to work. I shouldn't have been out so late last night, but it couldn't be helped. I had this perfectly timed. If I ran to work, I would make it there at exactly eight fifty-five. Five minutes early and Frank couldn't say a word to me. Five minutes to put my makeup on in the bathroom. I was notorious for being late and was put on warning more times than I could count. If I could quit, I would. But I needed this job.

As I ran past Freddie's fruit stand, Freddie yelled, "Running late again, Delilah."

"Like always, Freddie." I smiled.

I looked at my watch as I opened the door to the diner. *Yes!* It was eight fifty-five.

"We're busy, Delilah. Get moving," Frank said in a harsh voice.

"I have five minutes until my shift starts," I said as I flew past him and into the bathroom.

As I looked at myself in the mirror, I swept a champagne-colored shadow over my blue eyes and brushed my lashes with mascara. After sweeping a pink color across my cheeks, I dabbed my lips with some pink petal lip gloss. It was nine o'clock and I heard Frank yelling my name.

"Good lord, Frank. I'm right here," I said as I put on my apron and grabbed my order pad.

The morning rush finally ended and it was time to prepare for the lunch crowd.

"Delilah, I need to talk to you in the back, now!"

I rolled my eyes. "What is it, Frank?"

"You're spending too much time talking to the customers. They aren't here to chat up. They're here to eat. So take their order and move on. We need to get these people in and out as fast as we can. Time is money, Delilah, and I won't tell you again."

"Fine, Frank. I won't talk to the customers."

The lunch crowd was starting to stagger in and, once again, the race was on.

"Is Frank giving you a hard time again?" Daphne, the other waitress asked.

"When isn't he?" I smiled as I walked over to table number five and took their order.

The bells that hung above the diner door chimed, and when I happened to look over, a man in a suit – a very handsome man in a suit – walked in with a little girl. I walked to the kitchen and placed the order ticket on the ticket rack. When I turned around, I noticed they were sitting in my section.

"Hi, can I get you two something to drink while you look over the menu?"

His blue eyes looked at me. "I'll have coffee and she'll have milk."

"I want juice, Daddy."

"Correction. She'll have juice." He smiled.

I poured him some coffee and set the cup of juice with a lid on it and a straw down in front of the little girl. She was really cute with her long, blonde hair that sported light waves and her big green eyes.

"Are you ready to order?" I asked as I took my order pad from my apron pocket.

"I'll have a garden salad with Italian dressing and a cup of chicken noodle soup and she'll have the grilled cheese."

"Would you like French fries with that, sweetie?" I smiled at her.

"Yes, please."

"One salad, soup, and grilled cheese coming right up."

I placed the ticket up on the counter and attended to my other tables.

"That guy with the kid is fucking hot," Daphne said as she walked by.

"I know. I can't stop staring at him. I don't think I've ever seen a man so perfect."

"There's nothing sexier than a hot and sexy man with a kid." She smiled.

And he was sexy. He stood a little over six feet tall, had light brown hair that was perfectly styled short all the way around, and amazing sea-blue eyes. His concrete jawline and chiseled cheekbones defined him as godlike. While I was in my daydream, Frank rang the bell, alerting me that an order was up and ready. I walked over and put the food on a tray and took it over to his table.

"Here you go. One salad with Italian dressing and a cup of chicken noodle soup. And one grilled cheese with French fries for the little lady."

She giggled. "What's your name?" she asked.

"My name is Delilah. What's yours?"

"Sophie." She picked up a fry and took a bite.

"It's nice to meet you, Sophie."

I looked over at her dad and he was staring at me. "Delilah is a pretty name."

"Thanks." I smiled as I took my fluttering heart and walked away.

The diner was getting more crowded by the minute. After attending to some other tables, I walked back to the table where Sophie and her dad were sitting when she knocked over his cup of coffee.

"I'm sorry, Daddy." I heard her start to cry.

"It's okay, Sophie. It was an accident."

I ran to get a towel and, when I came back, Sophie was crying and throwing a bit of a temper tantrum. I wiped up the coffee as he wiped his pants with the napkin.

"It's okay, Sophie. It was an accident," I said to soothe her. But it didn't work.

"Sweetheart, please stop. It's okay." People around the diner were staring.

I sat down next to Sophie and began to sing. "The itsy bitsy spider walked up the water spout. Down came the rain and washed the spider out." She joined me. "Up came the sun and dried up all the rain, and the itsy bitsy spider went up the spout again." I ran my fingers up her arm and she giggled.

"Delilah! What did I tell you about the customers?"

"Frank, I was just calming her down. She's a kid, for God's sake."

"I'm done talking to you. That was the last straw. You're fired."

As I sat there and stared at that heartless son of a bitch, anger rose up inside me. I stood up from the booth, took off my apron, and threw it at him. "You can't fire me because I quit!" I went to the back, grabbed my purse, and stormed out of the diner. As I was walking down the street, I heard someone call my name.

"Delilah."

I stopped and turned around to see Sophie and her dad walking towards me.

"I'm really sorry about your job."

"Nah, don't be. Frank's an as—" I looked at Sophie. "Frank's not a nice man."

"Will you sing to me again?" Sophie asked as she looked up at me.

"Of course I will." I smiled as I bent down in front of her. I cleared my throat. "You are my sunshine, my only sunshine. You make me happy when skies are gray. You'll never know, dear, how much I love you. Please don't take my sunshine away."

"You sing pretty. Doesn't she, Daddy?"

"Yes, Sophie. She has beautiful voice."

"Thank you." I smiled.

After staring at me for a few moments, he reached in his pocket and pulled out a white card. "My name is Oliver Wyatt of Wyatt Enterprises. Can you stop by my office around four o'clock? I would like to talk to you about something." He handed me his business card. "The address is on the back."

Okay, this was strange. Why would he want to talk to me?

"Sure, but may I ask what you want to talk to me about?"

"You'll find out when you come to my office. I'll see you at four o'clock, Miss—"

"Graham. Delilah Graham."

He nodded his head as the corners of his mouth curved up and the two of them turned and walked the other way down the street. Sophie turned her head and gave me a small wave and smile.

Chapter 2

When I walked into my apartment, I found Jenny and her boyfriend, Stephen, fucking on the couch.

"What are you doing home?" she asked as she sat up and peeked at me from over the couch.

"I quit the diner. Well, Frank fired me first."

She pulled up her underwear and threw her shirt back on. Stephen pulled up his pants and looked at me.

"Bummer, Delilah."

I walked into my room and threw myself on the bed. Jenny lay down next to me and we both stared up at the ceiling.

"Why did he fire you?"

"For singing to a kid who spilled coffee and was crying."

"Bastard."

"I know."

"Hey, Jenny. I gotta go, babe. I'll see you later. Sorry about your job, Delilah."

"Thanks, Stephen. Sorry to interrupt your sex session." I smiled as I looked over at Jenny.

"It's fine. He was taking too long to come anyway." She grabbed my hand. "What are you going to do now?"

"I don't know. The weird thing is that the kid's father is Oliver Wyatt. He gave me his business card and asked me to stop by his office at four o'clock because he wants to talk to me about something."

"*The* Oliver Wyatt?"

"I guess. Is there more than one?"

"Not in New York. I've heard stories. When you get a chance, google him. I have to get ready and head down to the fruit market. The oranges must be restocked." She smiled as she got up and went to her room.

I sat up, opened up my laptop and googled Oliver Wyatt. God, was he hot. I was feeling things twitching down below that I never felt before just by looking at someone. I clicked on images and a bazillion pictures came up with him and different women. But the most recent pics were of him and some blonde

Barbie-looking girl. One of the captions read: "*Oliver Wyatt attends 'Home for Hope' event with girlfriend, Laurel Madison.*" All the women he was photographed with were gorgeous and filled with Botox.

I pulled out his business card from my purse and looked at the address. His building was on West 43rd Street. I looked at my phone. It was three fifteen. It would take about fifteen minutes to get there by cab, but at this time of the day, it might take longer. I went to my closet and pulled out my black cotton sundress.

"This will have to do," I said to myself. I didn't want to go to his office in jeans.

After changing, I pulled my hair from the ponytail and ran my fingers through it while I lightly sprayed it, giving it a bit of volume. I freshened up my makeup and slipped my feet into my low-heeled strappy sandals. Hailing a cab, I climbed in the back and told the driver to take me to West 43rd Street.

Nerves settled inside of me as I stood in front of the tall, glass building. As I walked through the large revolving door, I had to pass through security first before approaching the large, curved wooden desk that sat in front of a massive wall fountain.

"How may I help you?" the pretty blonde with her hair up in a tight bun asked.

"I have an appointment with Mr. Wyatt at four o'clock."

"Your name, please," she asked as she picked up the phone.

"Delilah Graham."

"There's a Delilah Graham here to see Mr. Wyatt. Appointment is for four o'clock."

She looked at me with her hazel-colored eyes. "Mr. Wyatt is ready to see you now. Just take the elevator to the right up to the twenty-second floor."

"Thank you." I politely smiled as I walked away.

Before I approached the elevator, the doors opened and I stepped inside. My stomach was in knots and I wasn't sure why. I was never nervous around people, but there was something about Oliver Wyatt that made me uneasy. Maybe it was his hotter than hell looks or maybe it was the way he seemed confident, controlling, and well poised. The doors opened and, as I stepped out, a woman with long black hair and shockingly red plump lips smiled at me.

"You must be Miss Graham." She got up from her seat and led me over to the oversized, dark stained wooden doors. She placed her hand on the lever and opened it, announcing my arrival. Oliver was sitting at his large, curved desk, which sat in front of a wall of floor-to-ceiling windows.

"Miss Graham, thank you for coming. Please have a seat," he said without so much as cracking a smile.

I took a seat in the leather chair that sat across from his desk as he sat down in his executive chair. I was nothing but a bundle of nerves as I gave him a small smile.

"I asked you here because I would like to know if you have any experience with children."

"Huh?" I asked in confusion.

He narrowed his eyes. "Do you have any education in child care, Miss Graham?"

"If you consider raising my three siblings an education in child care, then yes. As for formal education, no."

He cocked his head as he leaned back in his chair. "Please elaborate on that."

"Mr. Wyatt. Is this some sort of interview?"

"I guess you can call it that. Look, I need to find someone to take care of my daughter."

"You mean a nanny?"

"Yes."

"They have nanny services throughout New York you can call."

"Yes, Miss Graham," he said in irritation. "I know that and so far none of them have worked out very well. My daughter has some issues. She lost her mother recently and is having a hard time dealing with it. She can be a handful and the nannies that I've hired, she's driven to quit."

I raised my eyebrow. "And how old is Sophie? She can't be older than five."

"She is five and she has mind of her own."

I laughed. "Most girls do right from birth."

He didn't find that funny as he shot me a stern look. "Today at the diner, I saw something in the way she looked at you that I haven't seen with the other nannies. She seemed to like you and trust you, which I found comforting for her. I won't lie to you, Miss Graham. I did a background check on you. I know about you losing your mother at the age of eighteen and you becoming the legal guardian of your two brothers and sister back in Chicago."

"Wow. Okay. I guess you're a man who's in a position to find out anything about a person."

"Yes, I am, and I get the impression you are in desperate need of a job."

He was right. I was desperate and if he was offering me a job, I wasn't about to lie to him.

"I'd been taking care of Braden, Colette, and Tanner since I was a little girl. My mom was an alcoholic and she couldn't hold down a job. She drank all night and slept all day, leaving me to take care of the others because I was the oldest. So to fully answer your question, I have a great deal of child care experience."

"What about your father?" he asked.

God, this was embarrassing to tell someone like him. I took in a deep breath before answering his personally invasive question.

"The four of us had different fathers and my mom couldn't tell you who each of our fathers were."

"I see," he said as he raised his eyebrow. "How long have you lived in New York and why did you leave Chicago?"

"I moved here a year ago. My siblings are at various colleges now and I wanted to get out of Chicago. New York is the center of the universe as far as I'm concerned and an ever changing place to live. Plus my roommate already lived here, so I didn't have to worry about a place to stay."

"I see. So what else do you do besides waitressing? Have you ever attended college?"

"No. There wasn't time for college, Mr. Wyatt. I was too busy working and trying to take care of the bills and my brothers and sister. I made sure to set them on the right path of life and get a good college education. I love music and I love to sing. I guess you can say that I moved here because I felt closer to the music."

"Do you have any plans to attend college?"

I laughed. "I'm twenty-three years old. I think it's a little late for college."

"It's never too late, Miss Graham. Do you have a boyfriend?"

I narrowed my eyes at his question because, frankly, it wasn't any of his business. "No," I hesitantly replied.

"Here's my offer, Miss Graham. I will pay you a salary of $40,000 a year to start and I will provide you with health insurance. You will live in my home, where you will have your own bedroom and bathroom and access to my personal driver whenever you need him. You will work Monday to Saturday, starting when Sophie wakes up and until she goes to bed. Sundays are your own and you're free to come and go as you please as I have a fill-in for that day. But keep in mind that if I need you in an emergency, you are to be readily available. The job may call for an occasional trip, so I hope you don't mind flying."

"No, not at all." The only thing that was running through my head was the amount of money he was going to pay me if I accepted the position. I really had no choice. I needed a job and fast, plus he was paying for health insurance.

"Is this something you'd be interested in?" he asked.

I didn't want to seem desperate and take the job on the spot. "May I take the day to think about it?"

"Of course." He took a pen from his desk and wrote something on a post-it note. "Here is my cell phone number. Call me when you've made your decision."

"Also, I'm sorry about the loss of your wife."

He looked at me oddly and then his lips parted. "Sophie's mother wasn't my wife. She was a woman I had dated who got pregnant on purpose with the hopes that I'd marry her."

"Oh," I whispered as I looked down.

There was a knock at the door and, without warning, it opened. I turned around and, oh fuck, there was another sex God in the room.

"Oh sorry, Oliver. I didn't know you were in a meeting. Maria wasn't at her desk."

"It's fine, Liam. Miss Graham was just leaving."

"Yes. Yes, I was." I got up from my seat and put my purse over my shoulder.

"Hello, Miss Graham. I'm Liam Wyatt. Oliver's brother." The corners of his perfectly shaped mouth curved up.

"I'm Delilah Graham. It's nice to meet you."

"Believe me, the pleasure is all mine."

I smiled at him and quickly left the office. I couldn't get out of there fast enough before my ovaries exploded. Two of the sexiest men I'd ever seen in the same room was a bit much.

Chapter 3

Oliver

"Who the fuck was that delicious creature?" Liam asked as he sat down across from me.

"She's the girl that I'm hoping will accept the position of becoming Sophie's nanny."

"Damn, Oliver. Do you know what you're doing? If she worked for me, there would be no way I could keep my dick in my pants."

I sighed and walked over to the bar to pour a glass of scotch. "Scotch?" I asked him.

"Sure. Where did you dig her up?"

"She worked at the diner where I took Sophie today for lunch since the babysitter wasn't available until two o'clock. She got fired, because while Sophie was having one of her meltdowns, she sat down and sang to her. Sophie responded well to her and there was something about Delilah that she connected with. It was weird. I'd never seen her like that with the others."

"Maybe because the others were old bats and Delilah is a beautiful young woman. You're crazy if you don't think she's hot."

"Of course I think she's hot. Are you kidding me, I get hard just by looking at her and you should have heard her voice. She has the voice of an angel when she sings."

"So then, are you hiring her for Sophie or for you?"

"For Sophie, you idiot. I told you that she connected with her instantly."

"I don't think it's a good idea, bro, and I'd hate to see what Laurel says when she finds out."

"I don't give a damn about what Laurel thinks. It's none of her business who I hire to take care of my kid."

"Are you going to tell Delilah about Elaine?"

"No. There's no need for her to get into my business like that. She'd be Sophie's nanny and that's it. She doesn't need to know anything about Sophie's mother."

Liam sighed and got up from his seat, shaking his head. "Good luck. Let me know if she accepts the job because I'll be spending more time at your house."

"You stay away from her, little brother. Do you understand me?" I said with authority.

"And so it begins." He smiled as he walked out and shut the door.

I sat back in my chair and finished off my scotch as I thought about Delilah. The way her long, brown wavy hair fell over her shoulders and her sparkling blue eyes. How the first thing I noticed when she walked into my office was her long lean legs. Legs that I envisioned wrapped around my waist as I fucked her. Her slender torso and her beautiful cleavage, which peeked through the black dress she was wearing. I thought about how her tits would look as she stood naked before me. She looked to be a C cup, which was perfect for me. Were her nipples a rosy pink? I pushed the button on my desk and locked the door as I unzipped my pants and took hold of my rock hard cock, stroking myself up and down as I thought about her pussy. Did she shave completely or did she sport a landing strip? I bet she was really tight. She didn't seem like a slut who had slept with a lot of men. She came across as innocent and angelic. Maybe she was a virgin. Stroking myself faster, I envisioned her small, perfect round ass and how good it would feel to grab it tight as I fucked her from behind. The look on her face when I'd make her come and how good she would taste on my lips. I softly moaned as I released myself into my hand.

Chapter 4

Delilah

Before going up to the apartment, I stopped in at the fruit market and found Jenny stacking cucumbers. It was her dad's fruit market and Jenny worked for him while she attended NYU.

"Hey," I said as I handed her a cucumber.

"Hey. How did it go with Mr. Wyatt? What did he want to talk to you about?"

I bit down on my bottom lip. "He wants me to be Sophie's nanny."

She set the cucumber down and a look of shock swept over her face. "What the fuck? Are you serious?"

"Yes. Starting salary is $40,000 with health benefits and I would have a personal driver for me and Sophie."

"Would you live there?"

"Yeah. I would. I'd have my own bedroom and bathroom and Sundays off."

"Damn, Delilah. Are you going to take it?"

"I really have no choice. It would be a hell of a lot better than waitressing."

"What about your music?"

"I can practice there and play on Sundays. I think this is a good opportunity, at least for a while."

"And what happens when you become attached to Sophie?"

"I'll cross that bridge when I get to it."

"And what about Mr. Sexpot Wyatt?"

"What about him?"

"Are there any fringe benefits involving him that come with the job?"

"Stop it. I'm not like that and you know it. He'd be my boss and he has a girlfriend."

"So. Men like him don't care about their girlfriends if another beautiful woman enters the picture."

"Ugh. I'm going to go and get ready for tonight."

"Okay. Stephen and I will see you later." She laughed.

I went up to the apartment and changed out of my dress and into a pair of black leggings and a long black tank top with silver embellishments. I ran the brush through my hair and pulled it over into a loose side ponytail and threw a few curls on the ends. Slipping on my tall boots, I grabbed my guitar case, purse, and phone and headed out the door. As I sat on the subway, I decided to give Mr. Wyatt a call.

"Oliver Wyatt," he answered.

"Hi, Mr. Wyatt. It's Delilah Graham."

"Hello, Delilah. Have you made your decision about the position I've offered you?"

"Yes, I have and I accept."

"Excellent news. What's all that noise? Are you on the subway?"

"Oh yeah. Sorry about that. I'm on my way to the Red Room. I wanted to give you a call before it got too late."

"May I ask what you're doing at the Red Room?"

"I'm singing there tonight."

"Ah. I see. We can go over the details another time. Have a good night."

"Thank you, Mr. Wyatt. You too."

I ended the call with a smile on my face as I got off and walked a block to the Red Room. Walking through the doors, I spotted Jonah, a friend of mine I met when I first moved to New York when I played my guitar and sang on his corner.

"Hey, Delilah." He smiled.

"Hey, Jonah. It looks like quite a crowd tonight." I looked around at the room full of patrons.

"You're up next after Blue Moon and Stars. Are you ready?"

"All tuned up and ready to go." I smiled as I patted my guitar case.

I walked to the back of the stage area, took my guitar out, and as soon as Blue Moon and Stars exited the stage, I walked on and sat down on the stool in front of the microphone. The lights were bright and as I began to strum my guitar, all attention was on me. There was no place in the world that I felt more at home than I did on a stage, singing and escaping into a world where I was somebody; a world where I belonged. As I began to sing my acoustic cover of "Let Her Go," the Red Room quieted. I closed my eyes and sang, taking in the sound of the strings and baring my soul for the love of music. When I opened my eyes, staring out at the crowd of people, they locked on Oliver Wyatt's, who was sitting at a table in the corner with a drink in his hand. *What the hell is he doing here?* After singing a few more songs, I thanked the crowd and got up and walked off the stage. The sounds of clapping and whistling filled the air in the Red Room, alerting me of another successful performance. Setting my guitar in its case, I picked it up and walked out into the main area and headed to the now empty table where Oliver had just sat and watched my performance. Why would he just leave without saying anything? I shrugged and went up to the bar where Jonah was mixing drinks.

"Excellent performance, Delilah. This one's on me." He smiled as he set down a White Russian in front of me.

"Thank you." I picked up the glass and took a sip.

"Hello, beautiful lady." Stephen walked up and kissed my cheek. "Amazing performance as always."

Jenny sat down on the stool next to mine and hooked her arm around me. "Jonah, three shots of tequila, please."

"Coming right up, Jenny." He smiled.

I looked over at her while Stephen talked to a friend of his. "When I was up on the stage, I saw Oliver sitting at the table in the corner, watching me."

"Really?" She twisted her face in confusion.

"Yeah, but after the performance, he left. He didn't say a word to me or anything."

"That's weird, Delilah. Maybe he's some kind of millionaire stalker." She laughed.

"Well, if he is, he won't have to stalk me since I'll be living in his home."

"You already accepted the position?"

Jonah set the shots of tequila down in front of us. Jenny handed me a glass and then gave one to Stephen. "One… two… three!" she yelled as we threw back the shots and slammed the glasses on the counter.

"Yep. I called him while I was on the subway on my way here."

"I sure hope you know what you're doing, Delilah. You're going to be living in a whole different world."

I gave her a small smile and finished off my White Russian.

Chapter 5

I awoke to the sound of my phone buzzing. With the pillow over my eyes, I haphazardly fished around my nightstand for my phone. Grabbing it, I tossed the pillow over to the other side and saw that Oliver was calling.

"Hello," I said sleepily.

"Good morning, Delilah. Did I wake you?"

I looked over at the clock and it read nine a.m. "No. I've been up."

"It sounds like I woke you."

"No, no. I've been up for a while." I didn't want him to know that I slept this late. I was pretty sure that he was one of those who started his morning between four and five a.m.

"I'll be sending my driver, Scott, over to your place to pick you up. I'd like to tell Sophie together that you'll be her nanny, and I wanted to show you around so you can get acquainted. You can start moving your things in tomorrow."

"Tomorrow!" I gulped.

"Yes. Tomorrow is Sunday and you officially start working for me on Monday. Is that a problem, Miss Graham?"

"No. Not a problem at all, Mr. Wyatt. I can do that."

"Good. Please text me your address so I can give it to Scott. I'll have him come by in about an hour. Sound good?"

"Yes. An hour is fine."

"See you then." *Click.*

I threw back the covers and climbed out of bed. If only he would have stayed at the Red Room last night and told me about this instead of springing it on me at the last minute. I sighed as I stepped into the shower. As I was blow-drying my hair, Jenny walked in and sat down on the toilet.

"Where are you going so early?"

"Oliver is sending his driver over to pick me up so we can tell Sophie that I will be her nanny and he wants to show me around. Apparently, he wants me to move in tomorrow because I officially start working on Monday."

"Tomorrow? Gee, Delilah, that's like tomorrow."

"I know. How the hell am I supposed to get everything packed so quickly?"

"Just pack some things and leave the rest here. You'll be back visiting, so you can just take little bits at a time."

I pointed the hairbrush at her and smiled. "Good idea. I didn't think of that."

She got up from the toilet, hooked her arm around my neck, and gave me a light hug. "Have a good day and I'll see you later. Try to keep your panties dry while you're with Mr. Wyatt." She winked.

"Very funny."

I was going to miss seeing Jenny every day. She had been my best friend since we were seven years old when her family bought the house next door. We hung out every day and did everything together until her mom passed away and her dad decided to move to New York and open up a fruit market when she was sixteen years old. Distance didn't affect us. We talked every single day, sometimes all night long. She met Stephen about two years ago when he knocked over the display of apples all over the market floor. She said it was love at first sight and they'd been together ever since.

I left the apartment and walked down the stairs. A black limo was parked at the curb with a man standing with the door open.

"Miss Graham?" He smiled.

"Hi. You must be Scott." I held out my hand to him. "Just Delilah, please."

"It's a pleasure to meet you, Delilah."

I climbed in the back seat and smiled as I looked around at the plush black leather interior and ran my hand along the smooth leather seat. I'd never been inside a limousine before and I was liking it. Scott pulled up to the curb and I stared at the tall, single black wrought-iron gate with the fancy scroll design and pointed tips. Beyond the gate sat a beautiful stone staircase made up of ten stone steps and intricately designed handrails on each side that led up to the four-story reddish bricked home. As I approached the double dark stained wooded doors with the full-length beveled glass, Scott pushed the thumb latch down on the handle. Pushing the door open, he allowed me to enter first. I stood in the mammoth foyer and took note of the expensive-looking marble tile floor and the beautiful winding wood staircase that sat to the right. I had never seen such tall ceilings as I did when I looked up in that room.

"How tall are these ceilings?" I asked Scott.

"All the ceilings in the home range from ten to eleven feet."

"Wow." I was almost afraid to see the rest of the house.

"Mr. Wyatt asked that you take a seat in the dining room and wait for him. It's over here to your right."

I followed Scott as he led me to the oversized room where the floor-to-ceiling windows throughout gave the most perfect view of the beautiful gardens outside. The focal point of the room was the long mahogany-finished wood table with beautiful beige upholstered chairs. A large floral centerpiece made up of burgundy and cream flowers sat in the center of the table.

"Hello, Delilah." I heard Oliver's voice from behind. "Welcome to my home."

I turned around and gasped when I saw him standing there in a pair of dark wash jeans, a white button-down cotton shirt, and a brown sports coat. He looked even sexier out of his business attire. Thoughts of Jenny as she told me to keep my panties dry kept running through my head.

"Hello, Mr. Wyatt and thank you."

"You can call me Oliver."

I nodded as I gave this godly man a small smile.

"If you follow me, I'll show you the rest of the house and your bedroom. Sophie is out at the moment with my maid, Clara."

He led me through the door from the dining room that led to the large kitchen. The cherry cabinets, burgundy granite countertops, and marble floor gave the look of elegance. Over in the corner sat a round table that seated four people and another winding staircase.

"There are two entry ways to the second level."

The staircase led to a long hallway, which led to a massive living room where leather couches, loveseats, and chairs occupied the space as well as a large fireplace and one of the biggest TVs I'd ever seen. Floor-to-ceiling windows that overlooked Central Park blew me away. But the one thing, the one thing that excited me the most in the entire room, was the baby grand piano that sat in the corner by the windows.

"You have a piano," I said with a hint of excitement in my tone.

"Yes. You can play it any time you want. Now, follow me."

I followed him towards the back of the room where there was another hallway. To the right was a bathroom. To the left was a wall of closets and straight ahead was his office.

"This is my home office where I spend most of my time when I'm home."

"Is that all you do, Oliver? Work?"

He looked at me with a smirk. "Yes. I'm a very busy man."

"Sounds tedious."

He gazed at me for a few moments and then looked away, leading me up another flight of stairs.

"This is your room," he said as he opened the door on the left. "Go ahead and take a look around."

I walked inside and inhaled deeply. This room was bigger than my whole apartment. The walls displayed a deep taupe color that complemented the white moldings around the room. A beautiful deep purple and taupe patterned comforter graced the king-sized bed. The opposite wall contained a gas fireplace with a sixty-inch TV mounted directly above it. Each side of the fireplace contained built-in cabinets with drawers and shelves behind the doors. Sitting in front of three floor-to-ceiling windows sat a chaise lounge in the same deep purple as the comforter and a large desk sat in the corner. I could never leave this room and be completely happy.

"Wow. This is beautiful."

"I'm glad you like it. Around the corner is the large walk-in closet and the bathroom."

We walked down the hall and stopped at Sophie's room; a beautiful pink room fit for a princess.

"Okay. That concludes a tour of the house."

"What about your bedroom? Or don't you ever sleep?" I asked with a smile.

"My room is further down the hall and around the corner. But my room is off limits. The only people who are allowed in there are the maids."

"Okay." I nodded my head.

"Let's go into my office so we can discuss in more depth the job and your responsibilities."

Chapter 6

Oliver

I led Delilah back to my office and placed my hand on the small of her back as she entered the room before I shut the door. She looked pretty in her navy blue capri pants and blue and white striped short-sleeve sweater. Her brown hair was long and wavy and she was only wearing light makeup. She wasn't painted, she wasn't plastic, and she wasn't fake. She was carefree and she could sing like no one I'd ever heard before.

"Please have a seat," I spoke as I sat down behind my desk. "Sophie is a troubled child and she needs guidance. She can be physically abusive and she goes into fits of rage. She's antisocial and doesn't respond well with other children. I blame her mother for that."

"May I ask how long Sophie's lived with you?"

"Six months."

"But she's five years old. Obviously, you saw this problem before now since you're her father and you've helped raise her the last five years."

"Delilah. I never had much contact with Sophie prior to her coming to live with me. I didn't want children and her mother knew that."

She looked at me as confusion swept across her face. "Are you saying that you never saw her or spent time with her?"

"You need to understand that I am a very busy man. My work and my company take precedent over anything else."

"Sophie isn't a thing. She's your daughter, Oliver."

"Delilah. This is not up for discussion anymore. You are in charge of Sophie. You are to make sure her needs are met. Now, can I trust that you'll do just that?"

She looked down as she nodded her head.

"Excuse me a moment. I think Sophie and Clara are back." I got up from my seat and went down to the kitchen.

"How was your trip with Clara, Sophie?"

"It was okay."

Clara looked at me with a stern look on her face. "She had a meltdown in the middle of the store and then threw a jar of salsa on the floor."

"I'm sorry, Clara. Sophie, come up to my office with me. Someone is here to see you."

"Sorry, Daddy."

"Well discuss it later," I said in a stern voice.

She followed me to my office and smiled when she saw Delilah sitting there.

"Delilah!" She ran over to her and grabbed her hand.

"Hey, Sophie." She tenderly smiled and gave her a hug.

"What are you doing here?" Sophie asked.

"Sophie, I've hired Delilah to be your new nanny. She'll be moving in tomorrow."

Her face lit up as if she had just heard the best news of her life. "Okay. Can you teach me to sing?" She smiled at her.

"I sure can."

"Now go on up to your room and I'll be up shortly to discuss your punishment for your behavior with Clara."

She walked out of my office with her head down.

"What did she do?"

"Clara said she had a meltdown in the middle of the store and then threw a jar of salsa on the floor."

Delilah let out a light laugh. "Sorry, but I remember my sister doing that once."

"That type of behavior is inexcusable and will not be tolerated. I think I need to make an appointment with a therapist."

"Don't be rushing off and sending her into therapy, Oliver. She lost her mother and she's acting out. She's starving for attention and you need to find out what the root of her problem is. For my sister, it was my mom's lack of parenting and attention. Let me work with Sophie and see what I can do. Sometimes a little love is all it takes."

"I don't know, but if it doesn't improve, she's going into therapy. It seems that we're done here. I'll have Scott drive you home so you can start packing up your things for tomorrow."

I got up from my seat and was taken aback by her question.

"Why did you come to the Red Room last night, watch my performance, and then leave without saying anything?"

I leaned back on the edge of my desk and stared at her and her beauty. "I didn't have anything to say. I came because I was curious."

"Curious about what?"

"Your performance. You were very good. If you're going to be working for me and taking care of my daughter, I need to know who you truly are. I don't ever want there to be any surprises or some deep dark secrets that you may be keeping from me."

"I can assure you, Oliver, that I don't have any deep dark secrets or skeletons in my closet. I divulged all of my personal information to you during our interview. There's nothing else about me that you don't already know." She got up from her chair and began to walk out of my office.

I could tell she was irritated by what I had said. "Miss Graham." She turned around. "Thank you for being honest."

She gave me a small smile and nodded her head. I walked her to the front door and, as she walked outside, Liam was walking up the steps. He smiled and said hello to her before stepping inside.

"Hook, line, and sinker. You got her to work for you. I can say that I'm not surprised. Women love to be in the company of us Wyatt men." He smiled.

"Contrary to what you believe, Liam, she's my employee and that's all."

"Have you told Laurel yet?"

"Like I already told you, it's none of Laurel's business who I hire."

"If you say so. Are you ready to go play some golf?"

"Yes. Just give me a few minutes. I have to talk to Sophie first."

I walked up to Sophie's room and found her sitting on her bed, holding her Barbie doll.

"Why don't you tell me why you broke a jar of salsa?"

"I don't know." She pouted.

I placed my hand on her leg. "Sophie, that kind of behavior is unacceptable and you just can't do things like that. Do you understand that?"

"Yes, Daddy. I'm sorry." She reached up and wrapped her small arms around my neck.

I hugged her and kissed her head. "Promise me you won't do it again, sweetheart."

"I won't."

"Good girl. Daddy's going golfing with Uncle Liam. Clara is downstairs if you need anything. I'll be back later."

I got up from the bed and before walking out the door, I turned around and looked at my daughter. "I love you, Sophie."

"I love you too, Daddy."

Chapter 7

Delilah

When I walked into the apartment, I went straight to my room and saw a handful of boxes sitting on my bed. I sighed as I opened my closet and started packing my clothes. I was excited to be moving into Oliver's house and starting my job as Sophie's nanny, but I was also feeling conflicted about him. Why? I wasn't quite sure. He seemed very closed off in many ways, even where Sophie was concerned. Here was a little girl who had just lost her mother and had been shipped off to live with a father she barely knew. No wonder she was angry. I'd be too. Hell, I spent a majority of my life being angry for what my mother put me through. Then there was Oliver's brother, Liam. I got the impression he was more open than his brother. I packed what I could and set the boxes on the floor. As I went to the kitchen, Jenny and Stephen walked in with a few bags from the fruit market.

"Hey. You're back." Jenny smiled. "How did it go?"

"You should see his townhouse. It's enormous and has four floors. My bedroom is bigger than this entire apartment and, the best thing, Oliver has a baby grand piano."

"Wow. Sounds like you'll be living like royalty," Stephen spoke.

"How was Sophie?"

"Apparently, she had a meltdown at the store with the maid and threw a jar of salsa on the floor."

"Ouch. Sounds like you're going to have your hands full with that little girl," Jenny said with a worried look.

"Actually, she'll probably be a piece of cake. It's him I'm worried about."

"With any luck, you'll have your hands full of him." She winked.

"I don't think I like you talking about another guy that way." Stephen turned and looked at her as he was putting the fruit in the refrigerator.

Jenny slapped him on the ass. "You know I love you, goofball."

The three of us cooked dinner together and then I went to my room and played my guitar.

After getting out of the shower, I walked back to my room and heard my phone ringing. I picked it up from the nightstand. It was Oliver calling.

"Hello," I answered.

"Hello, Delilah. I would like to send a truck to your place to gather up your things. I'm assuming you have boxes."

"Yes, I have several."

"I will send Scott over to pick you up in about an hour and the truck will follow behind. Is an hour enough time for you to be ready?"

"Yes, Oliver, an hour is fine."

"Good. Sophie is very excited to see you. She's been talking about it all morning."

"I'm excited to see her too."

"I have to go out of town on an unexpected business trip so I won't be here when you arrive. I'll be back next Saturday. If you need anything, ask Clara or call my brother, Liam."

"Oh. Okay. Have a safe trip."

"Thank you, Delilah. Have a good week with Sophie."

I hung up and a feeling washed over that I wasn't so sure of. I couldn't believe that he was going on a business trip for a week and I wouldn't see him. Why did I care if I saw him or not? I shook my head and sighed. I slipped into a pair of skinny jeans and tucked in the front of my white cotton button-down shirt, leaving the back to hang out. I grabbed a pair of black Vans and began to carry the boxes from my bedroom to the front door.

"Well, this is it," I said to Jenny with a tear in my eye.

"It's going to be weird not having you around here." She hugged me.

"I know. But we'll see each other all the time still and we'll talk every day."

"Bye, Delilah." Stephen wrapped his arms around me and gave me a warm hug.

There was a knock at the door. When I opened it, two men were standing there.

"We're here to pick up some boxes."

"They're right over there." I pointed.

I grabbed my large Nike bag and carried it down the stairs. Scott saw me and immediately took it from me.

"Good day, Delilah."

"Hi, Scott."

Jenny and Stephen stood at the top of the steps and gave me a small wave. As I climbed into the back of the limo. I rolled down the window. "Love you guys!"

"We love you," they said in unison. "Good luck!"

Scott pulled away from the curb and I had a feeling I had just said goodbye to the only life I felt comfortable with.

****

Over the course of the week, I settled into my bedroom, got to know Clara and the rest of the staff a little better, and bonded with Sophie. She was a great little girl but burdened with anger and sadness. She was starving for love, much like I was growing up. The one thing I noticed about Sophie was that she was really smart for a five-year-old. She loved to read and to draw. I believed that was her escape from reality as music was mine. I asked her if her father ever read to her and she said only sometimes because he was always too busy.

I hadn't heard from Oliver all week. Not even a single call or text asking how Sophie was. As I walked into the living room, I found Sophie sitting at the piano.

"Whatcha doing, Sophie?" I sat down next to her.

"Will you play for me?" she asked with sadness in her voice.

"Of course I will." I placed my hands on the keys and began to play and sing.

****

Oliver

I walked through the door, set my bag down on the floor, and walked upstairs. I stopped when I heard the piano playing and Delilah singing. As she played, I stood there and listened. A feeling washed over me that I shouldn't have felt. The same feeling I had when I first saw her in the diner. When she finished playing, I softly clapped.

"Daddy!" Sophie screeched as she ran to me. I picked her up and gave her a big hug and kiss.

"Hello, darling. How was your week?"

"It was great. Me and Delilah had fun."

"Good."

Delilah got up and walked over to me. "Welcome home, Oliver."

"Thank you. It's good to be home. Sophie, it's late. Go get in your pajamas and I'll be up to tuck you in."

"Delilah tucks me in at night."

"Well, that's good. How about we both tuck you in?" I set her down.

"Okay."

I walked over to the bar and poured a drink. "Would you care for one?" I asked.

"Maybe after Sophie goes to sleep."

I looked at her and smiled. I couldn't help but notice how beautiful she looked as she stood across the room.

"Let's go tuck her in and then we can have a drink and you can tell me all about your week."

We both went up the stairs to Sophie's room and she was lying in bed waiting for us. Delilah walked over and sat on the edge of the bed, pulling the covers up over her.

"Good night, little one. Did you say your prayers?" she asked Sophie.

"Yes."

"Good. I'll see you in the morning." Delilah bent down and kissed her.

As soon as Delilah got up from the bed, I kissed Sophie on her forehead and told her good night. Delilah and I walked out of the room and headed back down to the living room.

"I'm going to get a glass of wine from the kitchen," she said.

I grabbed the glass of scotch I had previously poured and followed her down. I watched as she took a wine glass from the cabinet. When she reached up, her shirt lifted, exposing her taut, flat stomach. All I could think about at that moment was sliding my tongue around her belly button.

"Here, let me pour that for you," I said. Our fingers touched when I took the glass from her hand.

She looked at me and then quickly looked away. She had felt something. I knew she did.

Chapter 8

Delilah

My body tensed as his fingers brushed against mine when he took the glass from me. He poured me some wine and gazed at me when I took the glass from him and we touched again.

"How was your first week with Sophie?"

"It was good. There are few things I want to talk to you about."

He nodded his head and led me back up to the living room. He took the seat in the wingback chair while I planted myself on the leather couch.

"Sophie is an extremely smart little girl."

"Of course she is. Look at who her father is." He smirked.

I gave him a small smile as I ran my finger across the top of my glass. "I think you need to have her tested. She reads books that a five-year-old shouldn't know how to read. Did you know she could read?"

"I see her in her room with books, but I just assumed that she was looking at them. Not actually reading them."

His lack of parenting was really starting to irritate me.

"Sophie has a love for art. She loves to draw and she told me that she wanted to paint pictures. When I took her to the library the other day, she asked the librarian about art history books. It seems she's has a fascination with artists. She checked out books on Van Gough, da Vinci, and Monet."

"Odd for a child. Don't you think?" he asked.

"No. Not really. I think she needs to express her feelings through art."

"So what are you suggesting, Delilah?"

"I think Sophie should be enrolled in an art class."

"And you got all this by spending only a week with her?" He took a sip of his drink.

"Anyone who bothered to pay attention to her would see it." I could tell I had just overstepped my boundaries.

"Are you implying that I don't pay attention to my daughter?"

"She told me that when she asks you to read her bedtime stories you only do on occasion because you're too busy."

He got up from the chair and walked across the room, looking out the window. "Like I've told you before, Delilah, I am a very busy man."

"She's starving for your attention, Oliver."

"I love my daughter very much and if you're insinuating that I don't, you have just crossed a line with me."

"I'm not saying that you don't love her. I'm saying that she needs you to pay attention to her."

He turned around and looked at me. "You've been here one week and now you think you know everything there is to know about my daughter. I hired you to take care of her, not analyze her and certainly not to tell me how I should raise her. Now, if you'll excuse me, I've had a long day and I'm going up to bed. I suggest you do the same." He walked out of the room.

I sighed as I set my glass down and went up to my room. Maybe I did cross the line with him, but I didn't care. He had to be told that he needed to step it up a notch in the parenting department.

The next morning, I walked into Sophie's room and she was dressed, sitting on her bed and reading the Monet book from the library.

"Good morning, sunshine. Are you ready for breakfast?"

"Yeah." She jumped off her bed and took hold of my hand. As we stepped into the hallway, Oliver came around the corner.

"Good morning. Did you sleep well, princess?"

"Not really," she spoke in a sad voice.

He looked at me and I looked away. We went down to the dining room and sat at the table, waiting for Clara to bring out breakfast.

"Good morning, Wyatt clan and Miss Delilah." Liam smiled as he walked in, kissed Sophie on the head, and sat down next to me.

"Good morning," I replied. This was the first time I had seen Liam since I moved in.

Just as Clara set breakfast on the table, I heard a voice from behind. "Good morning, darling."

I watched as the blonde-haired woman from the internet kissed Oliver on the cheek and then sat next to him, glaring at me from across the table.

"You must be the new nanny. I'm Laurel, Mr. Wyatt's girlfriend."

"Her name is Delilah, Laurel," Liam spoke. She shot him a dirty look.

"It's nice to meet you." I smiled. Not. It wasn't nice to meet her. In fact, what the fuck was she doing here?

"Sophie, say hello to Laurel," Oliver commanded.

"Hi." She looked down and took a bite of her scrambled eggs. I got the feeling Sophie didn't care too much for her daddy's girlfriend.

"I had such a good time on our trip, baby." She reached over and touched his cheek.

I looked down at my plate of food because I couldn't stomach looking at the fake blonde anymore. He took her on his business trip. Maybe that was why he didn't bother to call and check up on his daughter. *Asshole.*

"I can't wait for our golf game with the Sullivans. It'll be good to see Barb again." Oliver gave her a small smile and then looked at me.

If he was going golfing with her and today was my day off, who was going to keep an eye on Sophie? I had an idea.

"Hey, Sophie. How would you like to go with me to the art museum today?"

Her face lit up. "Really? Can Daddy come with us too?"

"No, Sophie, he can't. Your daddy and I already have plans for today," Laurel spouted.

Oliver sat there and didn't say a word. A feeling of sickness overtook me, knowing he hadn't seen his daughter for a week and he chose to go golfing with that fake bitch instead of spending the day with Sophie, fully aware that it was my day off.

"I have nothing to do today, Sophie. Can I come?" Liam asked.

"Yes. If it's okay with Delilah."

"Is it okay with you if I tag along, Miss Delilah?"

Oliver shot him a fierce look of anger from across the table. I silently smiled inside.

"Of course you can come. It'll be fun." I smiled at him.

I finished my breakfast and got up from the table. "If you'll excuse me, I will go finish getting ready and then we can leave. Sophie, run upstairs and grab your sweater," I spoke as I walked up to my room. I grabbed my phone from the nightstand and sent a text message to Jenny.

"Hey. I have to cancel our lunch plans for today. I'm taking Sophie to the art museum."

"Is hot stuff Oliver going with you?"

"No. He has plans with his girlfriend. Apparently she went on his business trip with him."

"I understand what a shitty father he is. Have fun and we'll talk later."

As I slipped on my shoes, there was a knock at the door. "Come in."

Oliver stepped inside and closed the door. "What do you think you're doing?" he asked.

"What do you mean?"

"Today is your day off and you're taking Sophie to the art museum. Why?"

"I really didn't have anything else to do and I thought it would be good for her. It's something she'd enjoy. Why? Do you have a problem with that?"

"I don't. I was just curious and I already have someone coming to stay with her."

"Then I guess you'll have to call and tell her not to come today."

"I'm sorry I can't go, but Laurel and I had this golf outing planned for over a month."

"No worries, Oliver. I know what a busy man you are. I'll make sure Sophie has a great time." I picked up my phone from the bed and it fell out of my hand and to the floor. We both bent down at the same time to pick it up. His face was inches from mine as he stared into my eyes. I gulped as twinges of excitement fluttered down below. He handed me my phone, turned away and stood up, opening the door and walking out of the room.

Chapter 9

When we walked into the museum, I thought Sophie was going to lose her breath. She was so excited as she looked around and begged me to find the paintings by Monet.

"I do believe those would be in the European Paintings Department, which is this way." Liam pointed.

We found the area and stepped inside the room that displayed a lot of paintings by European artists. Liam was turning out to be a really nice guy. Did he have an agenda? I didn't know, but I was going to be on my guard. He was the same height as Oliver. They sported the same build and their facial features were about the same. The only difference was that Liam had more of a sandy blonde coloring to his hair.

"So what did you think of Laurel?" he asked.

"You want my honest opinion?"

"Of course. I'm very curious." He smiled.

"I think she's a self-centered, self-absorbed, stuck-up bitch."

Liam chuckled. "I think you've hit the nail right on the head." He bumped my shoulder.

"I take it you're not fond of Miss Laurel?"

"Not really. My brother can do better than her. She doesn't give Sophie the time of day and that bothers me."

"Much like Oliver, from what I've seen so far."

"He's trying, Delilah. It hasn't been easy since Sophie's mother passed away and she came to live with him. He doesn't know how to be a father and he's worried about her because of her behavioral issues."

"She's five years old. All five-year-olds have behavioral issues."

"Laurel actually tried to convince Oliver to ship Sophie off to Vermont to live with her aunt. But Oliver wouldn't hear of it."

"So he does have some redeeming qualities about him."

"He's a good guy. I think he's just a little misguided about life."

"What about your parents?" I asked.

"Our parents took off to Germany as soon as I turned seventeen. My father was born there and always regretted leaving. Once we were old enough to take care of ourselves, they packed up and left. Nice parents, huh? Oliver had just graduated from high school and I was in my senior year. They signed over their house to us and took off. Oliver was working as a caddy at a golf course and overheard one of the members talking about flipping houses and how much money he had made. He talked to me about it and we sold our house, moved into a small apartment, and used the money to buy and flip houses. Oliver made his first million by the time he was twenty years old. He's always been the smartest one in the family and even smarter in business. I went off to college, thanks to him, and by time I graduated with my MBA, he was buying and selling buildings and that's how Wyatt Enterprises was made."

"Is it your company too?" I asked.

"Yep. We share it 50/50. Don't ever mention my parents to him. He's a bit sensitive when it comes to them."

I looked over at Sophie, who was staring at the painting that Monet painted of his wife.

"That's a beautiful painting, Sophie."

"It's his wife. She looks so sad. Just like my mommy always looked."

I glanced over at Liam and he shook his head. Sophie walked over to another painting and we stood back.

"What was the relationship between Oliver and Sophie's mother?"

He looked over and gave me a small smile. "That's something you'll have to talk to him about."

We spent the day at the museum and Sophie's mind absorbed all the information about the paintings and artists. When we arrived home, I said goodbye to Liam and Sophie and I headed inside the house. Oliver came walking down the stairs.

"How was your day?" he asked Sophie.

"It was so much fun, Daddy. I wish you could have been there."

"Me too, sweetheart. I'm sorry. We'll go another time." He kissed the top of her head.

Sophie ran up the stairs and I went into the kitchen for a glass of water. Oliver followed behind.

"Laurel isn't here?" I asked casually.

"No. I dropped her off at home after golf. Do you have plans tonight?"

"Yeah. Actually, I do."

"How was Sophie at the museum?"

"She was great. Well behaved and in heaven with all the artwork displayed on the walls."

I wanted to tell him about the comment Sophie made about her mother, but I was afraid he'd get mad if I brought her up. So I didn't even bother. The impression I got in just the short time I'd been there was that there was no talking to Oliver about anything. It was his way or no way.

"I need to go and get changed for tonight." I began to walk away and Oliver lightly took hold of my arm. I turned around and looked at him.

"Where are you going? Are you going out with Liam?"

Now that shocked me. "I really don't think that's any of your business, Oliver. It's my night off." He glared at me, pursed his lips, and then let go.

After changing into my jeans and a t-shirt, I slipped into my Vans, grabbed my guitar case, and stopped by Sophie's room to say good night.

"Hey, buttercup. I'm going out for a while. I wanted to say goodnight."

She set down her book and held out her arms. "Have fun, Delilah. Sing pretty."

"I will. Be good while I'm gone. I'll see you in the morning." I kissed her head and left.

I opened the gate and walked down the street, hailing a cab and having the driver take me to Union Square. That was where Jonah and I would meet up occasionally and sing our hearts out for the good patrons of New York City.

****

Oliver

"Hello, Scott. Did you find out where she went?"

"Yes, Oliver. She's in the subway at Union Station, playing her guitar and singing with some guy."

"I'll catch a cab there. Wait for me."

"Will do."

I stood around the corner and watched the crowd of people dance and tap their feet while they sang the song "Jackson." I found myself moving to the beat of their music. She looked so beautiful with a wide smile on her face as she sang and played her guitar. I stood there for an hour while they sang together and then each of them sang solo songs. They finished their last song and then hugged and said goodbye. Was he her boyfriend? She said she didn't have one. Did she lie to me? All these questions were going through my head and they shouldn't have been. She put her guitar in the case and picked it up. She started to walk in my direction and stopped when she saw me standing there, smiling at her.

"Oliver. What are you doing here?" she asked in surprise.

"I came to watch you sing. Is that a bad thing?"

She shook her head. "How did you know I was here?"

"Scott told me," I answered with caution.

"So you had him follow me?"

"Maybe." She walked past me and started down the street. "Delilah, wait. Are you mad at me?"

She stopped in the middle of the sidewalk and turned around. "Yes, Oliver. I am mad at you. This is my night off. I expect a little bit of privacy."

I held out my hands to the side of me. "I'm sorry. I just wanted to watch you play. That's all."

"You can watch me at home. What I do on my night off is none of your damn business," she yelled and continued walking.

Shit. I really pissed her off. I didn't think she pissed off that easily.

"Delilah, please." I caught up to her. "Please say you'll have coffee with me."

"Now? And who's watching Sophie?"

"Sophie is asleep and Clara is there. Please. Let's go grab a cup of coffee together. There's something I need to talk to you about."

She rolled her eyes. "Fine. There's a diner around the corner."

We walked through the door and sat down in a booth by the window. The waitress walked up and took our drink order.

"I'll have a cup of coffee and a slice of cherry pie." She smiled.

"I'll have the same."

"You like cherry pie?"

"It's my favorite pie in the whole world."

"Mine too." Her grin widened. "So what did you want to talk to me about? Did I do something wrong?"

The only thought going through my head was how she could never do anything wrong. She was too perfect. I know nobody's perfect, but Delilah was. At least to me. Damn. I was starting to get hard.

"No, Delilah. You didn't do anything wrong at all. So far, you've done everything right."

"What do you mean?"

"I want to thank you for taking Sophie to the museum on your day off. It's all she talked about after you left. For the first time since she came to live with me, she seems happy."

"You're welcome, Oliver. We're going to tackle Sophie's issues one at a time."

The waitress brought us our coffee and set our cherry pies down in front of us. "Who was that guy you were singing with?" I asked.

"He's my friend, Jonah. We met shortly after I moved to New York City. I stole his music corner."

"Ah. He's a good performer as well."

"Yeah, he is. He and his boyfriend also bartend at the Red Room."

I let out a sigh of relief. He was gay. That was the best news I heard all night. As I watched her eat her pie, I couldn't help but imagine her beautiful lips wrapped around my cock and her big beautiful blue eyes staring up at me as she moved her mouth up and down my length.

"So did you have fun with Liam?" I asked to get my mind off her mouth.

"Yeah. He's a great guy."

"He didn't hit on you, did he?" I asked with seriousness.

She cocked her head and smiled. "What if he did?"

"If he did, then I'd kick his ass. My employees are off limits to him. He knows the rules."

"Does that rule apply to you too, Mr. Wyatt?"

What the hell was she doing? Why would she ask me that? Was she trying to be cute? Because if she was, she'd succeeded.

"Of course it does. But since I make the rules, I can change them at any time." I winked.

She had piece of cherry pie filling in the corner of her mouth. I wanted to reach over and lick it away with my tongue but instead, I reached across the table and gently wiped it away with my thumb. She instantly brought her hand to mine and stared at me as if she was unnerved.

"I'm sorry. You had some pie filling right there."

She lowered her hand. "Thank you."

I gave her a small smile. "If you're ready, we can get going."

"I'm ready."

We walked outside and climbed into the limo. When we arrived home, Delilah asked where we kept the aspirin.

"There's a bottle up in the cabinet next to the stove."

I followed her into the kitchen, and as I opened the refrigerator to grab a bottle of water, Delilah reached up in the cabinet but couldn't find the bottle. I came up from behind and stretched my arm up over her. My body pressed against hers as I found the bottle. She turned around and looked at me.

"Clara put it up high and far back so Sophie couldn't reach it. Hold out your hand." I shook two white pills out and gave them to her.

She was leaned up against the counter and it was taking all the control I had not to kiss her. To feel how soft her lips were against mine. We stared at each other for a moment; my heart beating faster than usual.

"Here." I handed her my bottle of water and backed away.

"Thanks." She softly smiled as she popped the pills into her mouth. She handed me back the bottle of water. "I'm going to go up to bed now to sleep off this headache."

"I hope you feel better." I wanted to tell her that the best cure for a headache was obscene and maddening sex, but I also wanted to gently press my lips against her forehead and make her feel better.

She began to walk away and when she reached the stairs, she turned around and looked at me.

"Thank you for the coffee and cherry pie. Next time, it's on me."

Chapter 10

Delilah

My alarm went off at six a.m. and when I opened my eyes, my headache was gone. I didn't fall asleep right away last night because I couldn't stop thinking about Oliver and how it felt when his body was pressed against mine as he reached for the bottle of aspirin and the look in his sexy eyes when he handed me the pills. My feelings were becoming strong in the short amount of time we spent together, feelings I'd never felt before about anyone. Actually, I wasn't really sure what was happening. All I knew was that every time he was near me or even in the same room, my heart beat a little faster and my body would tingle. I tried to imagine what he'd be like in bed. Was he gentle? Was he rough? I would bet my life on it that he would always have to be in control. I jumped out of bed because that was enough thinking about my boss that way. I needed to remember that I worked for him and took care of his daughter. The inappropriate thoughts I had needed to stop. Besides, he already had Cruella for a girlfriend.

I finished showering, got dressed, and went in to see if Sophie was awake. She wasn't. As I left her room and quietly shut the door, Oliver came from around the corner, looking fucking hot as hell in his dark blue tailored suit.

"Good morning. How's your headache?"

"Good morning. It's all better. Thank you."

He gave me a small smile. "Is she still asleep?"

"Yeah."

We walked down the stairs and I headed into the kitchen for a cup of coffee.

"Good morning, Clara." I smiled as I grabbed a cup from the cupboard.

"Morning, Delilah. Morning, Mr. Wyatt."

"Good morning, Clara. Is breakfast almost ready?"

"It's ready now. Go sit down and I'll bring it to you."

I poured Oliver a cup of coffee as well and took it into the dining room.

"Thank you, Delilah."

I smiled as I sat down across from him.

"What are your plans with Sophie today?" he asked.

"I'm taking her to a playgroup."

He took a sip from his cup and arched his eyebrow. "Good luck with that."

Just as Clara set down our plates, Liam strolled in with a wide grin. "Good morning."

"Hey, Liam."

"Little brother." Oliver nodded.

He took the seat next to me and asked Clara for some coffee. "Where's Sophie?" he asked.

"Right here." She giggled as she walked into the dining room and gave Liam a hug and kiss.

"How about your daddy over here?" Oliver smiled.

She walked over, gave him a smile, and wrapped her little arms around him. "Good morning, Daddy."

She took the seat next to me and we high-fived each other.

"Are you feeling okay, Sophie?" I asked with concern because she seemed a little pale.

"Yeah. I'm just tired still."

"Maybe you're growing. Growing is exhausting." I tickled her.

I caught Oliver staring at me from across the table. I could feel myself blushing. After we finished breakfast, Oliver and Liam left for the office. I told Sophie to go upstairs and get dressed because I was taking her to a playgroup. She seemed delighted and went up to her room. After helping clean up the breakfast dishes, I went to check on Sophie to see what was taking her so long. I opened the door to her room and found her asleep on her bed. I found it odd that she went back to sleep. We missed our playgroup, but that was okay. It was obvious that Sophie needed to get some rest. Maybe she had trouble sleeping last night. About three hours later, as I was sitting on the patio strumming my guitar, Sophie appeared.

"Hey, sweetie. How are you feeling?"

"I'm okay. Did we miss our playgroup?" she whined.

I gave her a small smile. "Yeah, but that's okay. We can go another day. It's gorgeous outside. How about we go to Central Park for a while? I'll call my friend, Jenny, and ask her if she'll meet us there. I'm dying for you to meet her."

"Okay. I'll go brush my hair."

I walked into the kitchen and asked Clara if she could pack a picnic basket for us to take. She obliged and I called Jenny.

"I was just thinking about you," she answered.

"You were? Why?"

"I miss you. I haven't seen you in a while."

"That's why I'm calling you. I'm taking Sophie to Central Park for a picnic. Would you like to join us?"

"Oh. Perfect timing. I'm just leaving the market now. When are you going?"

"We'll be leaving in a few. Meet us over on Cherry Hill mid-park in about a half hour."

"Sounds good. I'll bring the blanket."

"It better not be that one you and Stephen have sex on." I laughed.

"Very funny, Delilah. I'll see you in a bit."

Sophie came down, I grabbed the picnic basket and my guitar, and we walked outside where Scott was waiting for us. He dropped us off and I took hold of Sophie's hand as we walked to Cherry Hill. Her shoe was untied, so I set my guitar and the picnic basket down to tie it for her. She lifted up her pant leg and I noticed a large black and blue bruise on her leg.

"Sophie. How did you get that bruise?"

"I don't know. It just appeared."

I looked up at her strangely, tied her shoes, and when we got to Cherry Hill, Jenny was already there sitting on the blanket.

"Sophie, I would like you to meet my best friend in the whole world, Jenny."

"Hi." She smiled.

"Hello there, Sophie. It's nice to meet you."

We sat and had lunch and Sophie asked me to play the guitar. I did for a bit and then she went off to read her book underneath one of the cherry trees.

"So, how are things with Oliver?"

"Fine."

"Has he made a move on you yet?"

I sighed. "Why do you think that he's going to hit on me? He has a girlfriend."

"Have you met her?"

"Yeah. I nicknamed her Cruella." I laughed.

"She's that bad?"

"Yeah. I think she is. I can tell she doesn't like Sophie being around."

I looked over at the tree that Sophie was under, reading her book. She was asleep.

"That's odd."

"What?" Jenny asked.

"Sophie is sleeping again. We were supposed to go to a playgroup this morning, but she fell asleep on her bed."

"Maybe she's coming down with a virus."

"Maybe. I should get her home." I dialed Scott and asked him to come pick us up. "Can you take my guitar case and the basket while I carry her?" I asked Jenny.

"Of course."

I walked over to the tree, took the book from her hands, and picked her up. "Come on, princess. Let's go home."

Chapter 11

Sophie slept for a couple of hours and then came down to the kitchen, where Clara was teaching me a new chicken recipe.

"Hey, Soph. You okay?"

"Yeah. I'm thirsty."

Clara went into the refrigerator and poured her a glass of orange juice as Sophie climbed up on the barstool.

"Hey. Want to hear something fun?" I asked her.

"Sure."

I took the plastic cup that was sitting on the counter, clapped my hands, and began singing the Cup song. Sophie sat across from me and laughed. When I finished the song, I heard light clapping from the entrance of the kitchen. I looked up and Oliver was standing there with a smile on his face.

"Very cute, Delilah." He walked in and gave Sophie a kiss on the head.

"Thanks." I blushed.

"I have a surprise for you, pumpkin," he said to Sophie. "Follow me upstairs."

We went up to the living room, where there was an easel, canvases, paints, and supplies.

"No way, Daddy!" she exclaimed as she ran over to it.

"Now you can paint all the pretty pictures you want." He smiled.

"Oh, thank you, Daddy. I love you." She threw her arms around him.

"I love you too, sweetheart."

I stood back and watched her as she took out the paint brushes and examined each one.

"You just made her one happy little girl."

"I hope so. How did it go today at the playgroup?"

"We didn't go. When I went to go see what was taking her so long to get ready, she was asleep on her bed."

"Really?"

"Yeah. So we met my friend, Jenny, in Central Park and had a picnic. It was weird because Sophie went and sat under one of the trees to read a book and she fell asleep."

"Is she sick?" He looked at me with concern.

"She may be coming down with something. I don't know. I guess we'll have to wait and see."

"Well, let's hope if it's something, it doesn't last long. Oh, and just to let you know, Laurel will be coming to dinner and so will Liam."

"Okay. Is there a special occasion?"

"No, we were supposed to go out and talk about the event my company is hosting next week, but I wanted to stay home tonight. So I just had them come here."

"Does Cru—Laurel work for you?"

"No, but she's coordinating the fundraiser for us this year."

Wasn't she sweet? I rolled my eyes.

"Sophie, let's take your paints and stuff upstairs to your room and get you set up."

"Okay, Daddy."

I helped Oliver carry the stuff to Sophie's room and we set everything up in the corner by the window. It was the perfect place to paint. Sophie went and lay down on her bed.

"What's wrong, Sophie?" Oliver asked her as he sat down on the edge of the bed.

"I don't feel good, Daddy. My head hurts and I'm really tired."

He turned and looked at me with concern in his eyes. I walked over to the bed and placed my hand on her forehead.

"She's really warm, Oliver. Do you have a thermometer?"

"I don't know. I'll have to go ask Clara."

"Do you have any children's Tylenol?"

"I don't think so. Since Sophie's been with me, she's never been sick."

I sighed. "Then I'll have to run to the store and get some."

"No need. I'll send Scott. Tell me exactly what you need."

"A thermometer and children's Tylenol will do."

He walked out of the bedroom and I turned to Sophie. "You're going to be okay." I smiled down at her as I pushed back her hair. "Let's get you into your pajamas. You'll be more comfortable."

I got up from the bed and pulled her Ariel nightgown from the drawer. I helped her sit up and took off the clothes she was wearing. She slipped into her nightgown as I pulled back the covers and made her climb under them. A few moments later, Oliver walked in the room with the thermometer and Tylenol.

"That was quick."

"There's a drugstore on the corner," he said as he handed me the thermometer.

"Open up, Soph, and put this under your tongue." As soon as the thermometer beeped, I took it from her mouth and read it. "You, my dear, have a fever of 102.5. What's the dosage say on the bottle, Oliver?"

"One and a half teaspoons."

"Okay. Can you please pour that in the cup?"

I couldn't help but laugh as he struggled with the cap. He couldn't get it off.

"What the hell is up with this thing?"

"Give me it. It's a childproof cap." I immediately opened the bottle and poured it to the one and a half tsp. line. "Drink up, Sophie. You'll feel better."

She took the cup from my hand and drank it, making a sour face. I hurried and gave her the glass of water.

"Drink some water."

She took a few sips and then lay down on her pillow and closed her eyes. I kissed her on the head and Oliver did the same. As we walked out of the room, we left the door open slightly.

"Do you think she'll be all right?" he asked.

"She probably has a virus. We'll have to keep an eye on her temperature. She may need to go and see doctor tomorrow."

"She doesn't have a doctor."

"What?" I asked in surprise as we stood in the living room.

"She's never been sick. Listen, Delilah, I don't know the first thing about raising a kid. I'm taking this one day at a time. She never needed to see a doctor so why would I have one for her?"

"For instances like this! Plus, she'll need shots when she goes to kindergarten in the fall."

"Sophie will be attending a private school."

"So. You still need vaccines."

"Well, it's a good thing you're here, then."

I rolled my eyes. "I guess so."

As soon as we made our way downstairs, Laurel and Liam walked through the door.

"Hello, Oliver." She smiled as she kissed his lips. I wanted to puke. "Oh, hello, Delilah."

I gave her a small smile and then looked at Liam, who proceeded to give me a wink. Dinner was ready and being served in the dining room. I watched as Oliver placed his hand on Laurel's back and the two of them entered the room and sat down at the table. I couldn't stop thinking about last night and the way he wiped the cherry filling from the corner of my mouth. I took a seat at the table and Liam asked where Sophie was.

"She's in bed. She's sick."

"Poor kid. I hope she feels better soon."

"Thanks. Me too."

I caught Oliver staring at the two of us from across the table. It still bothered me that he asked if Liam had hit on me.

"So what kind of fundraiser are you doing?" I politely asked.

"It's for families of ALS and ALS research. We want to raise a considerable amount of money to help the families and give the rest for research," Oliver replied.

"That's nice." I smiled. "Do you pick a different charity every year?"

"Yes. As a matter of fact, we do." Liam grinned. "And every year is just as successful as the last."

"Do you think we can discuss the details?" Laurel snapped. "And, Oliver, may I ask why the nanny is having dinner with us? She's the help. Shouldn't she be sitting in the kitchen with Clara?"

"Be nice, Laurel," Oliver spoke.

I couldn't believe that bitch had just said that. Who the fuck did she think she was? Where I came from, back in Chicago, she wouldn't last a day. I was really pissed off that Oliver didn't stick up for me.

"She's here because she will be attending the fundraiser with me, so I want her involved in the details." Liam smiled. "Isn't that right, Delilah?"

I took a bite of my chicken as nerves settled inside of me, waiting for the volcano to erupt. "Yeah. I can hardly wait."

I looked up and over at Oliver, who was glaring at me. He didn't look happy. In fact, he looked downright pissed. Oh well.

"If you'll excuse me. I'll leave the three of you to discuss your business." I got up and took my plate into the kitchen. I needed to get hold of myself because that bitch was crossing the line with me. "How can Oliver stand that woman?" I spoke in rage to Clara.

She smirked. "She's a piece of work, isn't she? Don't let her get to you. One day, Mr. Wyatt will see her for who she truly is and kick her ass to the curb."

I smiled as I hooked my arm around her. "Thanks, Clara. I'm going to go and check on Sophie and then I'll be in the living room if you need me."

I walked up to Sophie's room and she was still sound asleep. I sat down at the piano and began to play and softly sing. As I finished my song, I heard the sounds of gentle clapping behind me. I turned around and Oliver and Liam were standing there.

"Well done, Delilah," Liam held up his glass.

"Thank you."

"Oliver, I have a wonderful idea. Why don't we have Delilah be the entertainment at the fundraiser?"

"I've already hired the band," Laurel snapped as she walked in the room.

"Then fire them," Oliver spewed. "I think that having Delilah sing at the fundraiser is a great idea."

"You can't be serious?"

"Yes, I am serious," Oliver replied.

"And so am I," Liam spoke. "So how about it, Delilah? Would you like to perform at the fundraiser our company is hosting?"

"I would love to." I smirked as I looked at Cruella.

She glared at me, and if looks could kill, I'd be dead. I didn't care. If Oliver and Liam wanted me to perform, then I would. It was for a wonderful cause and I was honored to be a part of it.

Chapter 12

Oliver

I walked over to the bar and poured myself another glass of scotch as Laurel continued to harp on me about having Delilah perform at the fundraiser.

"What the fuck is going on here?" she asked.

"What do you mean, Laurel?"

"Why are you catering to that little girl? Is it the way she looks at you, Oliver?"

"If you're talking about Sophie, then yes. She's my daughter and I will cater to her all I want."

"I'm not talking about Sophie and you know it."

"You're being ridiculous, Laurel. Delilah is my nanny and you need to stop this right now. She's a nice girl and she takes very good care of Sophie."

She walked over to me and ran her finger along my chest. "I'm sorry, darling. You know how jealous I can get when it comes to you. Why don't we go back to my place and fuck? I bought some new lingerie I'm dying to show you."

"As much as I'd love to, I can't. With Sophie being ill, I don't want to leave her."

Anger consumed her eyes. "Delilah is here with her. You don't need to be. She'll be fine."

"I said not tonight, Laurel. End of discussion."

Liam walked back into the room with a smirk on his face. "Are you two lovebirds having a disagreement?"

"I think Laurel was just leaving."

"Whatever, Oliver. I'll talk to you tomorrow." She grabbed her purse, and as she walked past Liam, she stopped and looked at him as he stood there eating a cookie. "I hope you choke on that."

She stormed off and Liam began to laugh. "She never did like me."

"Maybe because she knows you don't like her."

"What's to like?" He chuckled.

I poured my brother a glass of scotch and handed it to him. "What the fuck are you doing with Delilah? I warned you to stay away from her."

"Believe it or not, big brother, we're friends."

"Your intentions are more than that," I spewed.

"If you want to believe that, then go ahead. But I can assure you that as long as Delilah works for you, I know she's off limits and I know my boundaries."

"And what was that bullshit about you taking her to the fundraiser?"

"You wouldn't want her going alone, would you? Plus now she's performing there, so all is good. I know damn well Laurel would string you up by the balls if you brought her yourself and I secretly know you want her to attend."

"She's Sophie's nanny. I didn't have any intention of asking her to go. She takes care of my kid and that's it. Now who's going to stay with Sophie?"

He rolled his eyes at me and sighed. "You have another babysitter. Who's that girl? Francesca? She lives two doors down."

"She's Sundays only."

"Please. She'd love the extra cash and the few times she's been here, she and Sophie play nicely together. Now I have to go. I'll see you in the morning. Oh, and by the way, to ease your mind, I've met someone. Her name is Isabelle and I think I might like her." He smiled.

"Then why aren't you bringing her to the fundraiser?"

"Because she's going out of town to visit her sister in Pennsylvania. I'll bring her by one night so you can meet her."

"If that's the case, maybe we could double date," I spoke.

"Oh, you mean with me and Isabelle and you and Delilah?" He smirked. "Because if you mean you and Laurel, no thanks. I'd rather not subject Isabelle to her."

I sighed. "Get out of here. I'll see you in the morning."

As soon as he left, I went to Sophie's room to check on her. She was sound asleep. Delilah had disappeared shortly after we asked her to perform at the fundraiser and I wished she wouldn't have, but I got the impression that she wasn't putting up with Laurel. I silently laughed to myself because she was one tough cookie. I went to my bedroom, changed into a pair of pajama pants, and settled in for the night. As I opened my laptop and began to look over some emails, I heard Sophie screaming. I jumped up and by time I got to her bedroom, Delilah was already there, comforting her.

"What's wrong?"

Delilah turned and looked at me as she held Sophie against her chest.

"She says her ear is hurting really bad. I'll give her some more Tylenol. Go into the bathroom and run a washcloth under hot water. Ring it out and fold it."

I went to the bathroom and did exactly as she asked. Walking over to Sophie's bed, I handed Delilah the washcloth.

"Here, Sophie. Place this on your ear. Oliver, can you please get me a towel?"

"Sure." I grabbed a clean towel from the bathroom and handed it to her. She folded it and laid it on Sophie's pillow with the washcloth, telling her to lay her ear against it. I walked over to the other side of the bed and sat down next to Sophie, gently rubbing her back. "Just relax, sweetheart."

I couldn't help but take note of Delilah's pajamas. A pair of silk shorts and a matching tank top that was cut low in the front, accentuating her beautiful breasts.

"Looks like I'll have to take her to the clinic in the morning. After that, I'll find Sophie a good pediatrician," she spoke.

"Okay. I wish I knew of one, but I don't. Why don't you go back to bed? I'll stay with her for a while longer and make sure she's okay."

"Are you sure? I don't mind."

"I'm positive. Now go on." I gave her a small smile.

She got up from the bed, and my hard-on became even harder as I watched her walk across the room, her perfect ass barely covered by those shorts. There was no denying that I wanted her and I wanted to taste her badly. *Shit.* As soon as I made sure Sophie was settled and fast asleep, I went back to my bedroom and couldn't help but take care of myself, thinking about Delilah and that sexy body of hers.

Chapter 13

Delilah

It had been a long day. The doctor at the clinic confirmed that Sophie had an ear infection and put her on an antibiotic right away. After she ate an early dinner, I gave her a bath and then she said she wanted to lie down in her bed. It was seven o'clock when I heard the front door open and Oliver walked into the kitchen. He set his briefcase down and immediately undid his tie.

"Hello, Delilah. Is Sophie still up?"

"No. I gave her a bath and she said she wanted to lie down."

"Poor kid. I got the name of a pediatrician from one of the women at the office. She takes her son there and said he's wonderful."

"Great. I'll call and make an appointment for her to see him."

"Did Sophie eat dinner?"

"Yeah. Clara made her some chicken nuggets."

"Have you eaten yet?"

"No. I really haven't had the chance. Clara made pork chops. She didn't know when you'd be home, so she kept them in the warming drawer."

He frowned. "I don't feel like pork chops tonight. How about if we order some pasta from this great little Italian place around the corner?"

"Sure. That sounds good."

"Great. I'll call it in and go change." He smiled.

I took the plates from the cupboard, grabbed some silverware, and set the table. Clara had to leave early to do something with her family so it was only me and Oliver in the house, except for Sophie, who was sleeping upstairs. A few moments later, Oliver walked back into the kitchen wearing a pair of jeans and a navy blue t-shirt. He nearly took my breath away because I hadn't seen him dress so casually and he was sexy as hell. My body started to tingle and my heart picked up its pace.

"Grab a couple of wine glasses and I'll get us a bottle of wine."

As I set the glasses on the table, there was a knock at the door and Oliver brought the plastic bags into the dining room. As I served the food, he filled our glasses with wine.

"There's something I need to tell you. Sophie's Aunt Kelsey wants her to come stay with her and her husband at their farm in Vermont. It's about a five hour drive and she said that if I drive her there, she'll bring Sophie home because she wants to do some shopping in the city."

"How do you feel about that?" I asked as I sipped my wine.

"I think it'll be good for Sophie. They have a lot of animals on their farm and I think she'll enjoy it. Sophie and Kelsey are pretty close. She was Elaine's sister."

"Why don't you talk to Sophie in the morning and see how she feels about it?"

"I was planning on it."

I gave him a small smile as I ate my dinner. "This is really good."

"Isn't it? It's one of my favorite Italian places. You'd be shocked if you saw the place. It's a little hole in the wall with about ten tables total inside."

"Usually those kinds of places have the best food. In Chicago, there was this tiny little Mexican place a few blocks away from my house. They had the best Mexican food."

He poured himself another glass of wine. "Why don't you tell me a little bit about your childhood?"

"You already had me checked out, so there isn't much left to tell." I smirked. "The neighborhood I grew up in was run down and tough. There were a lot of drug dealings and gangs. But the one thing I can say is that no matter how bad things were, the neighborhood always took care of their own."

"And your mother?" he asked.

"She was a drunk and drank herself to death. She died of liver failure. As you already know, I was eighteen at the time. I spent my childhood raising and looking after Braden, Colette, and Tanner. Making sure they stayed out of trouble so they could get out and make something of themselves. I had to grow up pretty fast."

"It sounds like it. You said all three of them are in different colleges now?"

"Yeah. Braden is twenty-one and attending the University of Chicago. He's studying business and finance. Colette is nineteen and at the University of Florida studying to be a nurse, and Tanner, who's eighteen, is in his first year at Boston University studying journalism."

"You've done a good job. Sounds like they're living their dreams. Are they all on scholarships?"

"Yep. Scholarships and financial aid."

"And what about Delilah?" He smiled.

"What about me?"

"You have dreams too."

"Yeah, but my mom kind of took them away from me when she decided not to be a parent to any of us. My main focus was my brothers and sister. I've always wanted to live in New York and here I am. So, I'm living my dream."

He sat there and stared at me from across the table. "You are a very selfless person, Delilah. I admire that about you. I want you to know that."

I began to blush. "Thank you. So, it's your turn. Tell me about Oliver Wyatt and how you became the success you are at thirty years old."

"I'm sure my brother has already told you."

"Bits and pieces."

"So he told you about how our parents up and left us to move to Germany?"

I looked down because I sensed some bitterness in his voice. "Yeah."

"So then you already know about me. There isn't anything left to tell. I started out flipping houses and built up Wyatt Enterprises. Now I sell buildings and properties all around the world." He got up from his seat. "Why don't we go out on the patio and finish talking. It's a beautiful night out."

I got up from my seat as he grabbed our glasses and the bottle of wine and followed him out onto the patio, where we sat at the table in the large, cushy seats. He poured some more wine into my glass and changed the subject back to me.

"I bet growing up you had a lot of boyfriends."

"No. Not really. The longest relationship I'd ever had was about three days. I didn't have time for guys. I worked, took care of the kids, and had school. Guys couldn't be my main priority."

"And what about now?"

I looked at him strangely because I didn't know quite what he meant. "What do you mean?"

"Surely a woman like you has dated somewhat while you've been in New York."

"I went on a blind date once. Stephen, Jenny's boyfriend, set me up with one of his friends. It didn't go over too well."

"Why not?"

"He was a little on the strange side and he was high on our date." I laughed.

"Ah, nice first impression."

"What about you? Have you ever been in love, Mr. Wyatt?" I asked with a smirk.

He took another drink from his glass and sighed. "Does the age of seventeen count?"

"If you were in love, then yes."

"I thought I was. She was a great girl, or at least I thought so. We dated for over a year and did everything together. I gave her everything I had and possibly could. We had talked about marriage and building a future together. I even went as far as buying her an engagement ring for her birthday. One day, I went to her house after school to check on her because she told me she was sick and I found her fucking some other guy."

"I'm sorry."

"Don't be. Let's just say she turned me into who I am today. A man with a heart of stone and no desire to ever be put in that position again."

I knew this next question was probably teetering on the line of him telling me it was none of my business, but I had to ask anyway.

"What about Sophie's mother?"

"Elaine was a woman I had dated on and off. She was clingy, too attached, and wanted marriage. I made it very clear to her that it was never going to happen. She set out to get pregnant with the hopes that I'd have a change of heart and marry her. She was wrong. She tricked me, got pregnant on purpose, and then Sophie was born. I took the financial responsibility and paid her child support monthly and a good sum at that. She didn't have to worry about finances, believe me. A kid wasn't in my life plan and I resented Elaine for doing what she did."

My stomach tied itself in knots as I listened to him. "You never saw Sophie?"

"Nope. Not until she was three years old and Elaine showed up on my doorstep and introduced us. Elaine looked like she was strung out on drugs and she asked if she could come in. I told her fine and when she said she had to use the bathroom, she left for the day, leaving Sophie with me. I could tell right away she was a smart little girl. Elaine came back that night and said she did what she did with the hopes that I'd start being a father to Sophie. The truth was, I think she just wanted more money. I wrote her a check and saw Sophie a few times a year. Mainly on her birthday and holidays."

"But you took her in after her mother passed away."

"I'm her father. I really had no choice. I would be lying if I said that I wanted to. It was the right thing to do."

"Heart of stone, eh?" I smiled.

"Where Sophie is concerned, no. Everyone else, yes." He looked away.

I sat there and wondered about Laurel and the type of relationship they had. Did I dare ask him about her? No. It was none of my business. I was surprised he had even told me what he had.

Chapter 14

Oliver

I don't know why I told her everything I did. Maybe it was the fact that she was easy to talk to. I told her things Laurel didn't know. In fact, I didn't plan on opening up to her at all, but sitting across from her and staring into her beautiful blue eyes softened me and it felt right talking to her. I was waiting for her to ask me about Elaine's death and, sure enough, she did.

"How did Sophie's mother pass away?"

I took in a deep breath as I poured another glass of wine, looking at her intently, debating whether or not I should tell her. There were only two people who knew how she died and that was me and Liam. Nobody needed to know, especially Elaine's family.

"What I'm about to tell you stays between us. The only other person who knows is Liam. Do you understand?"

She narrowed her eyes at me and then said yes.

"Elaine died of an overdose of pills. Her family didn't need the burden of knowing that she killed herself. She was a Type 1 diabetic, so the coroner listed that as the cause of death, thanks to a generous donation I made to him."

"How do you know she killed herself and it wasn't an accident?"

"She left me a letter. Nice, eh? She apologized and told me to take care of Sophie and make sure she grew up well-adjusted and to give her everything she needs."

She reached across the table and placed her hand on mine. Her hand was soft and her touch sent electrical shocks throughout my body. *What the fuck?*

"I'm sorry, Oliver."

I pulled my hand away and got up from my seat, making the excuse that I had to use the bathroom. It was taking all the control I had inside of me not to grab her and kiss her. My body wanted her, and it was becoming unbearable.

"Thanks, Delilah. If you'll excuse me, I have to use the bathroom."

After getting my impulses under control, I walked back outside to the patio.

"It's getting late and we should call it a night."

"Good idea." She smiled. As she got up from her seat, she almost fell. I grabbed her arms to steady her.

"Be careful. I don't want you bruising that pretty face of yours."

"Wow. I think maybe I had one too many glasses of wine. Sorry about that."

"Don't apologize. It happens. Let me help you to your room." I put my arm around her and she laid her head down on my shoulder. I took in the scent of her hair, which smelled like flowers. I helped her up the stairs and to her room.

"Thank you, Oliver. Sweet dreams."

"You're welcome," I said as I stared directly into her eyes. "Sleep tight. I'll go check on Sophie, so don't worry. I'll see you in the morning."

I walked out and shut the door. Sweet dreams were the only dreams I'd have tonight, thanks to Delilah Graham.

****

Delilah

Confession. I didn't have too much wine. I knew if I stumbled, he'd help me, and I wanted to feel his touch, especially after I placed my hand on his. He said he had a heart of stone, but I didn't believe him. I saw someone different tonight. I saw a man who was capable of love and trust. I changed into my pajamas and climbed in bed, thinking about him and aching for more than just his arm around me. This was dangerous territory that I was embarking on. The type of territory that could hurt me something fierce, like he once had been. I had to put Oliver Wyatt out of my mind. He was involved with another woman and I wouldn't be the one to destroy that. Men with girlfriends and/or wives are off limits, no matter how bad my lust was for him. I needed sex. Maybe if I had sex with someone, my need would be satisfied and I wouldn't be feeling this way. What was this feeling? I didn't even know. I was confused and appalled at myself for even thinking about Oliver in a sexual way.

The next morning, Sophie came into my room and woke me up.

"I'm feeling better, Delilah." She smiled as I opened my eyes.

"That's wonderful, Sophie. But you're not a hundred percent yet. So you still have to take it easy."

"I'm hungry."

"Go downstairs and see Clara. I'll throw on some clothes and meet you down there."

She left the room and I got out of bed. I threw on a pair of yoga pants, a t-shirt, and put my hair up in a messy bun. It'd have to do for now. As I walked downstairs, Oliver was coming from his office. He stopped and looked at me.

"Are you feeling better?"

"I am. Much better. Thank you again for last night."

He gave me a smile as I walked ahead of him and down the stairs to the kitchen. I poured a cup of coffee and stopped dead in my tracks when I walked into the dining room for breakfast and saw Laurel and Liam sitting there.

"Good morning, sunshine." Liam smiled at me.

Shit. I looked like total shit.

"Good morning." I held up my coffee cup.

Laurel glared at me as I sat down, taking note of my morning look.

"Please excuse my appearance, but we all can't look as gorgeous as you in the morning, Laurel." I smirked.

Liam let out a light laugh and Oliver looked over at me. I could tell he was holding back the laughter.

"I think you look pretty, Delilah," Sophie said as she shot a look at Laurel.

"Little girl, that look you just gave me wasn't very nice. I suggest you learn some manners."

Oliver placed his hand on Laurel's arm. "That's enough, Laurel."

She huffed and pierced her fruit with her fork. I looked over at Liam, who was sporting a wide grin across his face. I lightly kicked him from underneath the table and he began to laugh.

"May I ask what is so funny?" Laurel said.

"I was just thinking about something. Relax, Laurel."

"Why don't you share it with the rest of us?" she asked in irritation.

"I can't. There's a child present."

"Okay, that's enough, you two," Oliver spoke. "Just finish your breakfast, Liam, so we can get out of here. Sophie, when I get home later, I have something I need to talk to you about."

"Okay, Daddy." She smiled as she ate her eggs.

Liam and Oliver left, leaving me at the table with Laurel and Sophie. Talk about an uncomfortable situation. I got up and took my plate into the kitchen. Sophie took her medication and then went upstairs to paint. As I was pouring myself another cup of coffee, Laurel walked in.

"I know what you're up to."

"And what would that be?" I asked as I cocked my head.

"You're turning Sophie against me and I don't appreciate it."

"I have no clue what you're talking about, Laurel."

She stepped closer and Clara looked at me. "Back off, Delilah. You may be the nanny, but that's all you are. Remember your place." She turned and the clicking of her heels on the floor made me cringe. As soon as she left the house, Clara and I busted out into laughter.

"Do you believe that bitch?" I asked.

"She's crazy. Don't let her scare you, Delilah."

"Scare me? Oh no, Clara. I can take her down in an instant."

I went upstairs to check on Sophie, who was sitting at her easel, painting.

"I'm going to take a shower, Soph."

"Okay. I'll be here, painting my picture."

"I can't wait to see it."

I blew her a kiss and went back to my room. I heard my phone ding. There was a text message from Liam.

"You're killing me with Laurel. Keep up the good work. I'm proud of you."

"Thanks. I try."

Chapter 15

Oliver

As I was sitting behind my desk, going over a proposal for an upcoming multi-million-dollar deal, my office door opened and Laurel walked in.

"Oliver, I've fired the band and they're pissed. They won't give the deposit back."

"Doesn't matter. Let them keep it for the inconvenience," I spoke as I stared at the computer.

She walked over to my chair and ran her finger along my shoulder for a moment before planting herself in my lap.

"Why don't we have a little office fuck?" She smiled as she unbuttoned her shirt and softly kissed my neck.

"Laurel, I—"

"Shh, baby." She placed two fingers over my lips. "I'm already wet and ready for you." Her lips brushed against mine as I cupped the back of her neck and forcefully kissed her.

My hand traveled to her breast as I pulled the cup to her bra down and took her hardened nipple between my fingers. She moaned as she got up from my lap and undid my pants, forcing her hand down the front of my underwear.

"What's going on, Oliver? You're not even semi-hard," she spewed.

"I'm sorry, Laurel. I've got a lot on my mind with this deal."

She stood up and buttoned her shirt. "Are you sure that's all it is?" She walked out of the office angrily and slammed the door behind her.

I rolled my eyes as I buttoned my pants. I didn't have time to deal with her right now. I pulled out my phone and sent a text message to Delilah.

"How's Sophie feeling?"

"She's feeling better. She's been painting all day."

"Good to hear. I'll be home in a while to talk to her about Vermont."

"Okay. See you soon."

As I set down my phone, Liam walked in.

"I just saw Laurel in the lobby and she looked pissed as hell. What did you do to her? I'm sure whatever it was, she deserved it." He smiled.

I sighed. "Nothing. She's overreacting as usual. Did you need something?"

"I talked to McAllister just a few minutes ago and he's ready to sign the deal for the sale of the building over on 77th. I got the price down like you wanted. We'll make a fortune off this building once it's restored."

"Ah, good." I smiled. "Best news I've heard all day. I told Delilah about Elaine last night."

"What? Why?"

I shrugged. "We were out on the patio, talking, and she asked. I don't know; it just felt right telling her."

Liam slowly nodded his head. "I see. Keep denying those feelings of yours, big brother. I gotta run. I'm meeting Isabelle for dinner. Keep your fingers crossed that I get lucky tonight." He winked before walking out of my office.

I shook my head and rolled my eyes. Shutting down my computer and placing the file in my briefcase, I left the office and headed home.

Delilah

I was on the phone talking to Jenny when Oliver walked in the living room.

"Let me call you back later. Oliver just walked in." *Click.* "Hey."

"Hi. You didn't have to hang up on my account." He gently smiled.

"It's fine. It was only Jenny."

"How come you haven't had her over yet?"

I twisted my face and cocked my head. "I don't know. Maybe because I work here."

"It's your home too, Delilah, and if you want to have your friends over, it's fine with me."

"Oh, in that case, can she come over tonight?"

"Of course she can. Now, let's go talk to Sophie."

I sent a quick text message to Jenny as we walked up the stairs.

"Come over tonight! I'm dying for you to meet Oliver."

"Sounds fun. What time?"

"How's seven?"

"I'll be there. Text me your address."

We walked into Sophie's room and I abruptly stopped when I saw her painting. I gulped. It was a painting of me in what looked like Central Park.

"Daddy!" she exclaimed as she hugged him.

"Hi, baby. Is that your painting?" he asked her as he turned and looked at me.

"Yeah. Do you like it? It's Delilah in the park," she said with excitement.

"Sophie, it's beautiful. Where did you learn to paint like that?"

"I don't know. I just know how. Delilah, do you like it?" She was beaming from ear to ear.

"I love it, sunshine." Tears started to fill my eyes. I couldn't believe she'd painted that.

"Look, you're holding your guitar. I can do a better guitar with more practice."

"It's beautiful, Sophie." I reached down and gave her a big hug.

Oliver sat down on the bed and asked Sophie to join him.

"Your Aunt Kelsey called and she would like you to come visit her and Uncle Matt at their farm in Vermont for a couple of weeks. How do you feel about that?"

"I remember going there once. They have horses and chickens and goats."

"Yes, they do. You can go horseback riding. I would drive you there and Aunt Kelsey said she'd drive you back home. But you'd be staying with them for a couple of weeks. They miss you."

"Okay. I miss them too. Can I bring my paints?"

He put his arm around her and squeezed her tight, kissing her on the top of her head. "Of course you can bring your paints."

"You're driving me?" she asked.

"Yes."

"Can Delilah come with us?"

Oliver looked up at me. "Sure. If she wants to."

"I'd love to drive with you to Vermont, Sophie." I smiled as I knelt down in front of her and took her hands.

"When am I going?"

"Once your ear infection clears up and you're feeling one hundred percent better."

"Okay. Can I get back to painting now? I have to add a few things."

Oliver and I both laughed. "Sure, sweetheart. We'll call you when dinner's ready."

I stared at the painting as I walked out of the room. I'd never seen anything like it before. Once we left the room, I grabbed Oliver's arm.

"That's not normal."

He looked down at my hand on his arm and then up at me with a grin. "I know."

"Oh, sorry." I let go of his arm.

"I think once Sophie gets back from Vermont, we should have her IQ tested."

"Good idea. Oh, by the way, my friend, Jenny, will be coming over around seven."

"Good. I can't wait to meet her." He smiled as he walked into his office.

Chapter 16

"Well, hello there, Miss Fancypants." Jenny smiled as she stepped into the foyer. "Look at this palace you're living in. Far cry from our Chicago days."

"No kidding." I laughed.

I showed her around the first level and then took her upstairs to the living room, where Sophie was watching TV.

"Hey, Sophie. How are you feeling?"

"Hi, Jenny. I'm feeling better."

I led Jenny to Oliver's office, where he had been since he came home.

"Oliver, this is my friend, Jenny. Jenny, this is Oliver Wyatt."

Oliver got up from his desk and walked over to where we were standing, extending his hand out to her.

"It's nice to finally meet you, Jenny."

"Thank you. It's nice to meet you too."

"Clara just informed me that dinner is ready. Shall we head downstairs?"

We walked out of his office and he walked over to the couch and took Sophie's hand. "Come on, sweetheart. It's time for dinner and then off to bed for you."

"Can I show Jenny my painting after dinner?"

"Of course you can. She'd love to see it." I smiled.

After finishing up dinner, I took Jenny up to Sophie's room to see her painting.

"That's beautiful, Sophie. Wow. You're very talented." Jenny turned around and looked at me with wide eyes.

As Sophie was showing Jenny her books, Oliver walked into the room.

"You go spend time with Jenny. I'll get Sophie ready for bed."

"Are you sure? It's no problem. I can do it."

"Go." He smiled.

I gave Sophie a kiss goodnight. "Don't forget to say your prayers before you go to sleep and I'll see you in the morning."

"Good night, Delilah. Good night, Jenny."

We walked out of her room and down to the living room. "Seriously, Delilah. What's up with Sophie? What child can paint like that at five years old? I can't even draw stick people." She frowned.

I sighed. "I know. Oliver and I are blown away. After she gets back from Vermont, we're taking her to have her IQ tested. I think she's like a genius or something."

We grabbed a couple of wine glasses and the bottle of wine that was left over from dinner and sat outside on the patio.

"So while Sophie's in Vermont, you'll be here alone with Mr. Sexpot?"

"Yeah. I guess I will be," I spoke as I raised my eyebrow. "It'll be good because then I can go out every night and play my music."

"That's a plus. Or maybe you can stay in and get some action." She winked.

I shook my head as I let out a light laugh. "There will be no action. He's my boss. But I do need to get laid. I've been thinking way too much about sex lately. Especially when he's around."

"Then give in to the temptation and fuck him. Get it out of your system."

"Yeah, right. I'm pretty sure that once you fuck Oliver Wyatt, there is no getting him out of your system."

She laughed. "I think you're right."

After talking for a couple more hours and a couple glasses of wine, she went home because she had an early class in the morning.

"Give Stephen a big kiss from me." I smiled as I hugged her goodbye.

I shut the door, grabbed my guitar, which I had left in the living room, and took it outside on the patio, shutting the door behind me. A few moments later, as I was playing the strings, the door opened and Oliver walked out onto the patio.

"It's late. Aren't you tired?"

"Yeah. I am. I just wanted to play for a bit."

"I like Jenny. She's nice and seems to have a good head on her shoulders."

"Thanks. She's the best."

"Well, good night. I'll see you in the morning."

As he started to walk away, I lightly grabbed his hand. He turned around with a startled look on his face.

"I just wanted to thank you for letting Jenny come over."

He wrapped his fingers around mine. I didn't expect that and my body caught fire.

"You're welcome. Like I said before, your friends are always welcome here. It's your home too." He softly smiled.

"Oliver, I—"

"Sweet dreams, Delilah." He let go of my hand and walked back inside the house, leaving me blown away by his touch.

****

A couple of days had passed and Sophie was feeling much better. As we were sitting at the piano together, pressing some keys, I had an idea.

"Wanna dance, sugar plum?"

"Yes! I love to dance!" she said with a wide grin.

I got up from the piano and set my iPhone in the docking station that sat below the TV. I pressed play on "Love Today" by Mika, one of my favorite dance songs. I looked at Sophie and held out my hand. We started dancing to the beat of the music around the room. As we were laughing, singing, and jumping around, suddenly, Liam joined us and grabbed my hand, twirling me around and pulling me close to him. He let go of me and grabbed Sophie, dancing around with her in his arms. I looked across the room. Oliver was leaned up against the wall with his arms folded, smiling at us. Next to him was Cruella, shaking her head in disgust as if we were doing something wrong. As soon as the song ended, Liam gave Sophie a kiss and put her down.

"That was one hell of a dance." He smiled at me.

Sophie giggled and ran up to hug Oliver. "You were amazing, princess. I love your moves."

"Why didn't you dance with us, Daddy? Uncle Liam did."

"That's because your Uncle Liam is way cooler than your daddy." Liam smiled.

"Don't kid yourself," Laurel said as she rolled her eyes.

"Oh, come on, Laurel. You know you want this big, bad—"

"Ahem," Oliver said as he looked at Sophie.

I couldn't help but laugh.

"In your dreams, Liam." She shot him a dirty look.

"You mean in my nightmare. Because that's exactly what it would be."

"Okay, that's enough!" Oliver shouted. "You two get in my office now. We have to discuss the fundraiser."

Laurel and Oliver walked away and I high-fived Liam. He strutted to Oliver's office with a grin on his face. A while later, as I was in the kitchen making a cup of coffee, the three of them came down the stairs.

"Make sure to save me a dance at the fundraiser Saturday night." Liam winked.

"I sure will."

"Come on, Oliver. Let's go," Cruella commanded in her wicked tone.

"I'll be going out this evening. If anything comes up with Sophie, don't hesitate to call."

"Everything will be fine. Have fun." I smiled. A fake smile. The smile that showed I was happy on the outside but sad on the inside.

I didn't want him to go out. I liked him being home. Even if he stayed locked up in his office, at least he was here. Watching Oliver Wyatt walk away with Laurel sparked a jealousy inside of me. A jealousy that shouldn't have been there. I was starting to feel lonely.

I went upstairs, helped Sophie get ready for bed, looked through her Monet book with her, and then sang her to sleep. When I entered my bedroom and closed the door, I decided to get in my pajamas and lie across the bed to watch a movie. Maybe watching *The Notebook* wasn't such a good idea. I sighed as I heard raised voices coming from downstairs. I quietly opened my door and stood at the top of the stairs while Laurel and Oliver argued.

"You can't stand there and tell me it's nothing else. We haven't had sex in what seems like forever."

"Is this why you followed me home, Laurel? We finished this discussion back at your place!"

"No we didn't. You walked out and left me standing there without any of my questions being answered. You obviously have a problem, Oliver. Maybe you should see a doctor."

"A doctor? Are you fucking out of your mind? I told you that I've been under a lot of stress lately with this deal. If it falls through, I'll lose millions. I'm sorry that I'm not up to performing for you."

"Bullshit! This all started when that nanny you hired moved in."

I covered my mouth with my hand. I couldn't believe I was listening to this.

"Jesus Christ, Laurel. Do you hear yourself? Why the hell would I be interested in her? She's Sophie's nanny and that's it. Are you jealous of Delilah or something?"

"No. Why would I be jealous of someone like her?"

"Well, you're basically accusing me of sleeping with her."

"It wouldn't be the first time," she said.

Oh. Shit. *Did he cheat on her?*

"It was one time, Laurel, and I was drunk. I apologized and you forgave me. I thought we put that behind us?"

"The fact that it happened will always be in the back of my mind."

"I think you'd better go before we both say something we're going to regret." His voice lowered. "The fundraiser is in a couple of days and we're both stressed out. Let's just get through this, okay?"

"Whatever, Oliver. I'll talk to you tomorrow." I heard the clicking of her expensive heels leaving the house.

I went back to my room and grabbed my guitar. As I strummed the strings, I couldn't help but feel hurt when I heard

Oliver ask Laurel why the hell would he be interested in me. He was right. Why would he be interested in someone like me? He was rich, powerful, successful, and sexy as fuck. I was a poor girl from a rundown drug-dealing neighborhood in Chicago. I'd misread his signals or possible intentions. I heard a light knock on my door.

"Come in."

"Hi. I heard you playing. I didn't think you were still up. Are you okay? You look like you've been crying."

"I just finished watching *The Notebook* and it gets me every time. No matter how many times I watch it, I still cry."

"I've never seen it."

"You've never seen *The Notebook*?" I asked in surprise.

"Nope. I don't have time to watch movies." He walked over to the bed and sat down next to me.

"Well, that's a shame, Mr. Wyatt, because movies are magical. I'm a movie freak."

"Maybe someday I'll get around to watching it. How was Sophie tonight?"

"She was great. You know, she hasn't had any behavioral problems since I started living here."

"I've noticed that. We can talk more about it tomorrow. I'm exhausted and had a long day. Sleep tight, Delilah." He walked out of the room.

"Sweet dreams, Oliver," I whispered.

I set down my guitar and climbed into bed. My mind was still reeling over the argument I heard between Oliver and Laurel. I was still in shock that he had cheated on her. After what he had experienced when he was seventeen years old and the hurt and pain he felt, I couldn't believe that he would turn around and do that to someone else. Maybe he wasn't the man I thought he was.

Chapter 17

Oliver

I stepped into the shower and sighed as I thought about Laurel and our fight last night. I wasn't in any mood today to talk to her and I knew she'd be blowing up my phone soon enough. After putting on my suit and tie, I walked downstairs to the kitchen and poured a cup of coffee.

"Morning, Clara."

"Good morning, Mr. Wyatt."

"Are Delilah and Sophie up yet?"

"We sure are." Delilah smiled as she and Sophie walked into the kitchen.

"Hi, Daddy."

"Good morning, Miss Sophie." I picked her up and gave her a kiss.

The three of us went and sat down in the dining room for breakfast.

"Delilah, the fundraiser tomorrow night is black tie. Do you have a formal dress to wear?"

She looked at me as she bit down on her bottom lip. God, was she beautiful.

"No. Nothing formal. I'll call Jenny later and ask her. I'm sure she has something."

I reached into my pocket and pulled out my credit card. "Here. Take this and go buy a new dress today."

"No, Oliver. I can't."

"You can't or you won't?" I asked as I cocked my head.

"I won't let you buy me a dress for the fundraiser. That's ridiculous. I can buy my own dress. Thank you."

"Take the card. Now," he commanded. "It's not up for discussion. Besides, I think Sophie needs some new clothes." He gave her a wink.

She giggled. "I want to go shopping with you and look at pretty grown-up dresses, Delilah."

She looked at Sophie and then at me with narrowed eyes. "Fine." When she took the card from my hand, our fingers lightly touched and I felt my cock twitch. "Buy a dress, jewelry, and a pair of shoes. Remember, you're going to be performing in front of a large crowd."

"Can I come, Daddy?" Sophie asked innocently.

"Sorry, sweetheart, but this is for grownups only. Francesca is going to come and play with you tomorrow night while we're gone."

"Okay. I like Francesca." She smiled. "But not as much as you, Delilah." She reached over and touched her hand.

"Aw, baby. I love you." She leaned over and touched Sophie's nose with hers.

Hearing her say those words to my daughter was bittersweet. Delilah was a godsend and I was happy that I'd found her. *Thank you, Sophie, for acting up in the restaurant and getting her fired.* I finished up breakfast and then headed to the office.

****

I finally closed the multi-million-dollar deal and I was ecstatic. To celebrate, Liam and I went to the golf course.

"Laurel told me that the band is still going to be there at the fundraiser, but they won't play until after Delilah performs."

"What?"

"You didn't know?"

"No. She didn't tell me that. But we haven't been getting along lately." I swung and nailed a hole in one.

"Damn you, Oliver." Liam sighed. "Why haven't you been getting along? Besides her being a bitch and all."

I looked over at the smirk on his face and rolled my eyes. "Let's just say I haven't been able to perform well in the bedroom lately. I've been under a lot of stress with this deal."

"Really? Or would a beautiful and sexy girl named Delilah have something to do with that?"

"Now you sound like Laurel. She basically accused me of sleeping with her and then she brought up the time I slept with Avril."

"You know, bro, and don't get pissed off at me for saying this, but have you told Laurel that you love her?"

"No. You know I don't tell anyone that besides Sophie. You know I can't find it in my heart to love another woman after what happened with Kristen."

"Seriously, Oliver, why are you still with her if you don't love her?"

I sighed. "I don't know."

"You were seventeen. Don't you think it's time to let that go?"

"I did let it go, but it's hard to trust again and I'm not sure I ever will."

"Well, if you want my honest opinion, I think Delilah is different from anyone else. She seems very trustworthy and I think you have strong feelings for her."

"I don't have feelings for her. I just want to fuck her and I don't want your opinion, little brother. So back off."

"All right. I'm backing off."

****

Delilah

As Sophie and I were in the dress section of Saks Fifth Avenue, looking at the beautiful dresses, I heard a voice behind me.

"Looking for a dress for the fundraiser?"

"Hi, Laurel. Yes. I am."

"Hello there, Sophie." She smiled at her with a fake smile.

Sophie looked down. "Hi," she whispered.

"Hey, Soph. Do me a favor and go look on that rack right there and see if any pretty dresses catch your eye for me."

"Okay."

I wanted her away from Laurel because I couldn't risk her telling her that Oliver gave me his credit card.

"I see you've gotten your dress." I pointed to the white garment bag hanging over her shoulder.

"Yes. I did."

"May I see it?" I asked politely.

"No. You may not," she said with an evil smile.

"Alrighty then. It was nice to see you, Laurel. Now if you'll excuse me, I have some shopping to do."

"You're not excused and I'm warning you, nanny. You better stay away from my boyfriend. Do you understand me?" she spoke through gritted teeth.

This was getting interesting. "I don't know what you're talking about and I don't want to know."

"Oh, you know damn well what I'm talking about. I see the way you look at Oliver like some schoolgirl slut who has a crush on her hot and sexy teacher. He's mine and you better keep your hands off of him or I'll make your life a living hell. You're nothing but white trash from the wrong side of the tracks."

I swallowed hard, and if Sophie wasn't there, I would have punched Laurel in the face already. But I needed to keep my cool and remain calm. She wasn't worth it. She was only making herself look stupid.

"Okay, Laurel. I fully understand what you're saying and you have nothing to worry about with me. I'm not interested in Oliver whatsoever."

"You better not be." She turned, said goodbye to Sophie, and walked away.

"Was she being mean to you?" Sophie asked.

"No, sweet girl. She wasn't being mean. We were just talking. Now let's go find a dress."

That would be the last time Laurel threatened me.

****

Oliver was in his study when Sophie and I came home from shopping. We were gone longer than anticipated, but we had dinner and then stopped at Central Park for a while. She was anxious to get home and start painting. I lightly tapped on his office door and he told me to come in.

"Here's your credit card."

"Thank you. Did you find something to wear?" he asked with a slight smile.

"I did. I also ran into Laurel at Saks."

"Oh. Everything okay?"

"Of course. Why wouldn't it be? She's a lovely woman."

Oliver stared at me and I could tell I amused him. "I take it that she must have said something to you."

"Just a friendly hi." I smiled. I wasn't about to tell him what I really thought of her. If he couldn't see what kind of person she was, then that was his problem and own stupidity.

"Can I see the dress you bought?" he asked.

"Sure you can. Tomorrow when I put it on." I winked and walked out of his office.

"Delilah, wait!" Oliver spoke.

I turned around and went back to his office. "Yes."

"I closed that big deal today."

"Congratulations, Oliver. That's wonderful."

"Thanks. Liam and I are going out to celebrate in a bit. Would you like to come with us? Maybe you can give Jenny a call and she and her boyfriend can meet us. We'll go hit up a bar."

"What about Sophie?"

"I'll ask Clara to stay. She will. Especially if I give her a bonus for doing it."

"I really should stay home and practice some songs for tomorrow."

"You don't need to practice. You're a natural. Come with us. It'll be fun."

As I stood there and stared at him, I bit down on my bottom lip, contemplating whether or not it was a good idea. But going to a bar with my friends sounded fun.

"Laurel isn't going?"

He chuckled. "No. She's busy tonight. So you and Liam both don't have to worry about her."

"Okay. I'll go. It sounds fun."

A wide smile splayed across his face. "Excellent. I'll call Liam and talk to Clara."

"And I'll go get ready." I smiled as I turned and walked up to my room.

Chapter 18

We met Jenny and Stephen at The Pony Bar in Hell's Kitchen. I had been here once before and really enjoyed the different beers they had.

"Do you want a beer?" Oliver asked me as the waitress walked over to our table.

"Sure. Whatever's on tap is fine." I smiled.

Oliver took the seat next to me and Liam sat across the table next to Jenny and Stephen. As soon as the waitress brought us our drinks, I held up my glass.

"I would like to make a toast. A big congratulations to Oliver and Liam for closing a huge deal today."

"Thank you." Oliver held up his glass.

"Here. Here!" Liam exclaimed.

Jenny looked at me sharply from across the table. "I need to use the restroom. Are you coming with?" she asked.

"Sure." As I got up from my seat, I placed my hand on Oliver's shoulder. "Place an order for the tempura green beans while I'm gone."

"You like those?"

"Love them!"

He gave me a smile and I followed Jenny to the bathroom. She grabbed my arm and pulled me inside.

"What the fuck is going on with you and Oliver?"

"Nothing. Why?" I asked in confusion.

"I see the way he looks at you and it's not in an employer/employee way."

I looked in the mirror and dabbed some lip gloss on my lips. "You're crazy. I ran into Laurel today at Saks. She threatened me and told me to stay away from Oliver."

"Did you deck her?"

"I would have if Sophie wasn't there." I smiled. "I wish you could meet her so you'd know what I'm talking about."

"I'm sure I will someday. But Oliver Wyatt wants you. I can tell and I know you secretly want him. Shit, Delilah. I don't know how you've managed not to jump in bed with him already. He's so yummy, and that brother of his. Wow!"

I rolled my eyes. "We better get back out there." When I opened the bathroom door, Liam was leaning up against the wall. "Shit. Why are you standing there like that?"

"I came to warn you. Laurel is here and she's sitting in your seat."

"What the fuck? How did she know we were here? And Oliver told me she was busy tonight."

"Obviously, the bitch changed her plans."

I sighed. "Twice in one day is not cool."

"What do you mean?" he asked.

"I saw her today at Saks and she threatened me. She told me that I'd better stay away from Oliver or else she'd make my life a living hell. She told me that I acted like a schoolgirl slut." I began to laugh.

"Are you serious? Did you tell Oliver?"

"No, and please don't. I can handle little Miss Cruella. She doesn't scare me."

"I have no doubt you can. Go back first. I'll join you in a few. I don't want anyone suspecting we talked about this."

I placed my hand on his arm. "Thanks for the heads up, Liam."

"You're welcome, Delilah."

"Looks like I'm finally going to get to meet that bitch." Jenny smiled as she hooked her arm in mine.

We walked back to the table and my stomach churned when I saw her and her arm around Oliver. I took in a deep breath to keep calm.

"Hi, Laurel." I smiled as I grabbed my beer that was sitting in front of her. Oliver looked at me and his eyes told me that he was sorry. She looked up at me and said hello.

The table we were sitting at only had enough room for five people. I could have very well gotten angry and stormed out of the place, but I wasn't about to give Laurel that grand satisfaction. Did it bother me? Of course it did. But I was here, having a good time with Jenny and Stephen. Oliver could spend the rest of the evening with Laurel for all I cared.

"We can squeeze in a chair right here." Liam smiled as he walked back to the table and pulled a chair up next to Oliver. "Hope you don't mind me getting too close, big brother?" He winked at him. "Delilah, go take my seat."

"Thanks, Liam."

He flashed me his sexy smile. The waitress walked over and set down the plate of tempura green beans in the center of the table.

"What on earth is that? It looks disgusting," Laurel sneered.

"Tempura green beans. It's what we poor folks from Chicago like." Jenny grinned as she popped one in her mouth.

I almost lost it and busted out into laughter. I flagged down the waitress and ordered another beer. Watching Laurel hang all over Oliver was nauseating. She was making sure that I knew he was her man. She reached over and placed her hand on his face.

"Congratulations, baby, on closing your deal. Now that it's settled, we can go back to my place and do some real celebrating later." She kissed his lips and, instantly, I felt sick to my stomach.

I pretended not to notice as I continued to smile, laugh, and drink my beer. I wasn't drunk but I was a bit tipsy. Nothing I couldn't handle. It was getting late and Oliver suggested that we leave. I gave Jenny and Stephen a hug goodbye and, as they left, Oliver touched my arm.

"I need to take Laurel home, so Liam is going to make sure you get home."

I hailed a cab as he was talking to me. "No need. I'm a big girl who can take care of herself. Enjoy the rest of your evening, Oliver."

I got into the cab before he could say a word, and locked the door. I turned my head the other way and told the cab driver to hurry up and pull away. I didn't know what I was feeling. I didn't know if I felt angry, sad, or disappointed. All I knew was that I wanted to go home, go to bed, and forget this night.

****

Oliver

"Way to go, Oliver. I'll be by tomorrow to pick up Delilah for the fundraiser." Liam got into his limo and left.

"Come on, baby. Take me home and fuck me senseless."

I pulled out my phone and sent a text message to Liam.

"Call my phone, now."

We climbed in the back of the limo and I told Scott to drive us to Laurel's apartment. My phone rang.

"Yeah, Marcus," I answered. "What?! Are you kidding me? Now? Do you see what time it is? Why didn't you call me earlier? Fine. I'll meet you there."

"What was that all about?" Laurel asked in disappointment.

"Marcus said there's a problem with the contract for the deal. I have to meet him now to get it straightened out before the buyers see it. Shit. I'm sorry, Laurel, but I can't stay at your place tonight."

"You can come by after, can't you?"

"I don't know how long I'll be and I need to be home in the morning when Sophie wakes up. I'm sorry, darling."

"Whatever, Oliver. This is getting old real fast."

My phone beeped with a text message from Liam.

"Good job, bro. See you tomorrow."

Scott pulled up to Laurel's apartment building and she got out in a huff, walking away without saying good night. What the hell was I doing? Why was I still with her? I didn't love her, I wasn't in love with her, in fact, half the time, I couldn't stand being in the same room with her. I needed to end things and fast. All I could think about was the look on Delilah's face when she got into that cab. She was angry, I could tell. She had the same look on her face that she had when she came back from the bathroom and found Laurel sitting in her seat. If that damn fundraiser wasn't tomorrow, I would have told Laurel to leave and ended things with her right then and there. She had no business showing up the way she did and I knew she only did it because Delilah was there.

I walked up the stairs and straight to Delilah's room. I lightly knocked and prayed she was still awake. I needed to apologize to her.

"Come in," I heard her say.

When I opened the door, she walked from the bathroom and looked at me. She was so fucking sexy standing there in her pajamas.

"Oliver, what are you doing here? I thought you were at Laurel's?"

"No. I dropped her off and came home. I wanted to apologize to you for tonight."

She walked over to the dresser and picked up a bottle of lotion. "There's nothing to apologize for."

I stood there, frozen for a moment. She was so innocent and sweet. I couldn't hold back anymore. The beast inside me erupted as I hastily walked over to her and grabbed her face, smashing my mouth into hers, tasting and feeling the softness of her beautiful lips. I had just crossed the line.

Chapter 19

Delilah

It happened so fast. His lips on mine, slipping his tongue inside and me letting him. I reciprocated at first, but then I pushed him away. I didn't want to. I didn't want his lips to leave mine, but it wasn't right. He looked at me as shock swept across his face.

"I'm sorry, Delilah. I didn't—"

I put my hand up and turned away. "Don't. Don't apologize. We went out and had too much to drink. It's the alcohol, Oliver, and I get that. That can never happen again. I'm sorry."

"You have nothing to be sorry for. I'm the one who fucked up."

"You didn't fuck up. Please don't think that." God, this was killing me and my eyes were starting to tear up.

"I don't want things to be awkward between us because of this."

"They won't be. Go to bed. Sleep it off and we'll pretend this never happened. I promise. It won't be awkward."

"Good night, Delilah." I heard the door shut and I turned around, holding my fingers to my lips, which were still pulsating from his feral kiss.

I climbed into bed, almost shaking from the feeling that overwhelmed me with just the mere touch of his lips. I wanted him, and if I would have let him continue, we would have had mind-blowing sex. I know we would have. I didn't want to stop it, but I had to. He had a girlfriend, maybe not a nice girlfriend, but he still was with her and I would be known as the girl he had cheated on her with. Plus, he was my boss and I needed this job. What if we slept together and things changed?

I had a fear of relationships. As I grew up, my mom gave me that fear with all the different men she slept with and getting pregnant by four different guys. I don't ever remember my mom having a boyfriend. She said relationships were toxic to the soul because they changed people. Thinking back on it, look at what it did to Oliver and how it changed his views. Did I ever truly believe what my mom said? I think subconsciously I did and that was why I wouldn't date anyone long enough to find out for myself. I had never depended on anyone to take care of me. I was the caregiver my whole life and I was fine with that.

The next morning, I opened my eyes and looked at the clock. It read eight fifteen. I jumped out of bed, threw on a pair of yoga pants and a t-shirt, and flew down the stairs to find Sophie.

"Clara, where's Sophie?" I asked in a panic.

"She's out with Mr. Wyatt. They went down to the bakery to get some fresh bagels. Are you okay, Delilah?" She poured me a cup of coffee.

I sat down at the table and put my hand on my forehead. "Yeah, I'm fine. I didn't mean to sleep this late."

The front door opened and Sophie ran into the kitchen, throwing her arms around me. "You're up." She smiled.

"Yeah. I'm sorry, Soph. I didn't mean to sleep so late."

"It's okay, Delilah. We got in late last night." Oliver gave me a small smile.

"Me and Daddy walked down the street and bought bagels with cream cheese."

"Did you have fun?" I asked as I pushed a strand of her hair behind her ear.

"Yeah. Do you want one?"

"Maybe later."

Oliver set the plate of bagels on the table. "They're still warm. That's when they're the best. You should have one now."

"Thanks. Maybe I will." I reached for the salted bagel.

****

Oliver

I tried to play it off as if nothing happened last night. As if I never kissed her and that it was all a dream. But the truth was, I did kiss her and it was a kiss that I would never forget. I wanted more of her. I needed more of her. To be inside her and make her come was my only desire. As the day went on, I worked in my study and didn't see Delilah the rest of the day. When I walked upstairs to take a shower and get ready for the fundraiser, I stopped outside her door and listened to her sweet angelic voice as she sang a song and strummed her guitar. I was nervous about tomorrow. We'd be driving Sophie to Kelsey's house in Vermont. Sophie being in the car would ease things, but the five-hour ride home alone with Delilah would be awkward.

I went to Sophie's room and stepped inside. "Are you all packed for Aunt Kelsey's?" I asked her as she moved the paint brush up and down the canvas.

"Yes, Daddy. See? There's my suitcase." She pointed to the corner of the room.

I sat down on the edge of the bed and asked her to come sit on my lap. She did as I asked and looked up at me with her beautiful green eyes.

"Are you sure you want to go tomorrow? Because if you don't, I can tell Aunt Kelsey you're not ready."

"It's fine, Daddy. I can't wait to see the horses." Her grin was wide.

"Okay, but if at any time you want to come home, you are to call me. Deal?"

"Deal." She wrapped her arms around my neck and gave me a hug.

The door opened and I gasped when Delilah stepped inside in her evening gown.

"Oh, I'm sorry. I didn't know you were in here."

Sophie jumped up from my lap and ran over to her. "You look so beautiful," she said. "Daddy, look at Delilah."

"I am, princess." I smiled.

Her black, sleeveless silhouette gown with the beaded side panel took my breath away. The way the dress hugged her hourglass figure and accentuated her five foot nine frame aroused me. The way her brown hair lay in soft waves over her shoulders made my cock rise even faster. I gulped as I stood up and placed my hand in my pocket, trying to control myself.

"Well?" She smiled. "What do you think?"

"It's a beautiful dress and you look very pretty."

"Thank you. The best part," she said with a wide smile, "it was on clearance."

I let out a light laugh. "I better go and get ready. Liam will be here soon to pick you up."

She gave me a small smile as I left the room.

Chapter 20

Delilah

Watching Oliver help Laurel from the limo made my stomach churn. His limo pulled up to the Waldorf Astoria a few moments after Liam's did.

"You nervous?" Liam asked as he grabbed my hand.

"A little."

"Don't be. You'll do great and everyone will love you. Are you going to be on your best behavior tonight where Laurel is concerned?"

"I'll try, but if she starts anything, I'll finish it." I smirked.

"Well, if that happens, make sure I'm around. I'd love to see you take that bitch down."

We got out of the limo and Oliver turned and looked at me as Laurel hooked her arm in his.

"We got this." Liam winked as he held out his arm for me.

We entered the grand ballroom and I was speechless. From the opulent lightening, floral arrangements, and white covered tables, I felt like I was transported into another time. Liam and I walked over to where Oliver and Laurel were standing. If she was trying to make it obvious that she was looking me up and down, she did a good job.

"Hello, Laurel. You're looking mighty spiffy this evening." Liam smiled.

"Shut up, Liam." She scowled.

Her strapless red dress was stunning. Too bad she ruined it by wearing it. The guests started to pour in. About three hundred of them, to be exact. I had invited Jenny and Stephen to attend and to represent her father's fruit market. She said they would love to donate to such a worthy cause. She walked in and Stephen wasn't on her arm; Jonah was.

"Hey, you two." I leaned over and gave them each a hug.

"Stephen has the flu. So I asked Jonah to accompany me."

"Bummer about Stephen. But bringing Jonah was an excellent choice." I smiled.

Oliver walked over to me and lightly took hold of my arm. "If you'll excuse me, I need to steal this beautiful lady for a moment."

"Sure. We'll catch up later."

"I just wanted to tell you that you'll perform after dinner. We'll be eating in a few minutes. I'll make a speech and then introduce you."

"Okay."

"Are you okay? Are you nervous?"

"I'm good. I'm always a little nervous before a show. Nothing I can't handle."

He smiled at me and then led me over to the table where we were seated for dinner. He sat down across from me, next to Laurel, and I sat next to Liam. There were two other couples sitting with us from Wyatt Enterprises. After finishing a five-course meal, Oliver got up and made his speech for the night with Liam and I went to the side of the stage. As soon as the clapping began and I was introduced, I stepped onto the stage with my guitar and began to perform. My nerves had finally settled after the first couple strums of my guitar. I prayed to God that people would enjoy my performance. As soon as I started to sing, the room quieted. After performing a few songs with the guitar, I moved over to the piano and began to sing my cover of "Let Her Go" by Passenger and a few other songs. I had a fun idea, so after finishing my last song on the piano, I stood up while everyone clapped.

"I would like to do something fun and introduce you to my friend, Jonah, who is an amazing musician. Jonah, will you join me up on this stage? If you're a Johnny Cash fan, sing with us and show us your dance moves."

He walked through the crowd with a smile on his face and jumped up on the stage. I handed him my guitar and we performed the song "Jackson." The attendees began to dance and everyone was having a great time. Once the song was over, the crowd whistled and clapped. Jonah and I took a bow and walked off the stage. Liam walked over to me and picked me up, hugging me and swinging me around.

"That was fucking amazing! You had these people moving." He smiled.

"Thank you."

I looked across the room as Oliver stood there and stared at me with a grin across his beautiful face. As soon as Liam put me down, I gave Jonah a hug and thanked him.

"No problem, Delilah. You know I love doing gigs with you." He kissed my cheek.

Jenny was drunk as she stumbled over to me. "Super duper amazing!" She held up her hand and we high-fived.

"I think I better get Jenny home. She's wasted."

"Good idea." I laughed.

I gave her a hug and told her that I'd call her. The guests were starting to leave and I looked around for Oliver. I didn't see him anywhere and I didn't see Laurel. I asked Liam where the restrooms were and he escorted me because he needed to use them as well. As we entered the hallway, I saw Oliver and Laurel standing there arguing.

"Uh-oh," Liam spoke.

"Just ignore them."

But being Liam, he couldn't. "So what are you two lovebirds fighting about now?" he asked.

"Get the fuck out of here, Liam. We don't need you putting your two cents in, Laurel shouted.

That made me angry. "Don't talk to him like that." The Chicago girl was emerging and I didn't care where we were.

"Can the two of you please just go?" Oliver asked.

"Don't you ever tell me what to do, nanny!" Laurel snapped.

I took in a deep breath and turned around, walking away slowly. Liam wasn't giving up.

"Are you seriously going to let her talk to us like that?" he asked Oliver.

"You heard your brother; take your fucking whore and get out of here."

I stopped. That was it. She had been pushing me for far too long and her choice of words at that moment was the straw that broke the camel's back. I turned back around and didn't even stop to think about the consequences of my actions.

"You've called me a whore for the last time, bitch!" I yelled as I decked her right across the face and she fell against the wall. "Shit!" I yelled as I shook my hand in pain.

Oliver and Liam stood there in shock as they stared at me. Liam busted into laughter and took hold of my arm.

"Let's get you some ice for that hand." He turned around and looked at Oliver. "Someone needed to put that bitch in her place."

We walked back to the ballroom and he grabbed a bunch of ice from the pitcher and wrapped it in a towel from behind the bar. He led me out to the limo and, as soon as we got inside, he placed the towel over my hand.

"You, Delilah Graham, are amazing and full of surprises. Did you see the look on her face? God, I wish I would have videotaped that."

I didn't say a word because I was ashamed of what I had done, but she pushed me. I would assume that, as of tomorrow, I would no longer have a job. There was no way Oliver was going to condone me hitting his girlfriend.

"Take some aspirin for the pain and get some sleep." Liam smiled as he helped me out of the limo.

"Thank you, Liam." I gave him a friendly hug.

"You're welcome. You better get up to your room before Oliver gets home."

"Do you think he's pissed?"

"He shouldn't be. If he is, then he's nothing but an asshole. She had it coming. I would have done it myself many times over, but it's wrong to hit a woman. Unless it's a woman hitting another woman." He smiled.

I went to the kitchen, got a new batch of ice, and wrapped it in the towel. I wasn't home ten minutes and Oliver walked in. *Shit. Shit. Shit.* He came into the kitchen and stood there with his hands in his pockets.

"How's your hand?" he asked.

"It's fine."

He walked over to me, picked me up, and set me on the counter.

"Let me see." He removed the towel and examined my swollen knuckles. Then, bringing my hand up to his lips, he softly kissed each one.

My heart was racing faster than the speed of light. What was he doing?

Chapter 21

Oliver

I wanted to take her pain away. I softly kissed each of her swollen knuckles as she stared at me. Placing her hand on her lap, I leaned in and brushed my lips against hers. There was no more holding back. I needed to fuck her and, this time, she wasn't stopping me. Her soft lips parted as my tongue entered her mouth, greeting hers as they tangled in delight. My hand grasped the nape of her neck, deepening our erotic kiss. She pulled back and stared at me.

"Do you have any idea how bad I want your body?" I asked breathlessly. "How bad I want to be inside of you? You're so beautiful, Delilah, and I need to fuck you," I pleaded.

"You have a girlfriend, Oliver."

"Not anymore I don't. I broke it off before I sent her home."

"Then do it," she whispered as she stared into my eyes and ran her finger across my lips.

I lifted her from the counter and took her hand, leading her up the stairs and to my bedroom. I shut and locked the door behind me as she walked across the room. I took off my bowtie and unbuttoned my shirt, while she slowly took down the straps of her gown and let it fall gracefully to the floor. She stood there in nothing but a pair of black lace panties, her nipples hard from the excitement that was about to come. I slid my shirt off and tossed it on the floor while slowly moving towards her. She was perfect and exactly how I imagined. She had the body of a goddess and I was going to explore every inch of her. I got down on my knees and softly kissed her stomach, running my tongue in circles around her belly button, with my hands planted firmly on her hips. She moaned and I became more excited. I'd been wanting her since the first day I saw her and now my fantasy was becoming a reality. Reaching up and firmly grasping her breasts, my mouth went farther down until it reached the top of her panties. As I kneaded her beautiful perky and natural breasts, she took down her panties. I gasped as her perfectly shaven pussy stared at me.

"Fuck, Delilah. You're so beautiful," I whispered as my tongue circled her clit.

She let out a moan and placed her hands on my head. She wanted this just as badly as I did, which turned me on even more. Before getting in too deep, I stood up and passionately kissed her lips while picking her up and then laying her down on my bed. My mouth traveled to her breasts, licking and sucking on each hardened peak. Moving downwards, I spread her legs and placed my face between her thighs, taking in the wetness and excitement before me. Her quiet moans were almost making me come. Placing my lips on her clit, I plunged my finger inside of her, causing her to arch her back in ecstasy. She tasted better than I imagined and I needed to thrust my cock inside her immediately.

****

Delilah

His mouth over my slick opening was more erotic than I had imagined. The roll of his tongue against my clit was sending vibrations throughout my body. My heart was racing and my breathing was shallow. He was magical. Not only with his mouth, but with his strong hands as well. This was what my body had been craving.

"I want to feel your cock in my hand, Oliver," I said with bated breath.

"You will. But first, you're going to come."

He pulled his finger out and moved his mouth down to my wet opening, flicking his tongue in and out at a rapid pace. His thumb pressed against my clit, making small circles as my body began to shake and I climaxed as never before, leaving me even more breathless.

"Perfect." He smiled as he stood up and undid his pants, sliding them off his hips along with his underwear and releasing his incredibly hard, long, thick cock. I gulped. It was perfect and just how I imagined it would be. I sat up, took hold of it in my hand, and listened to his erotic moans as I stroked his entire length and gently placed my other hand on his balls.

"Oh my God," he moaned. "I need to be inside of you now."

I lay back down and he hovered over me, his lips trailing across my neck before taking each nipple into his mouth as he sucked and lightly nipped them. He reached over to his nightstand and opened the drawer, pulling out a condom. The tear of the wrapper jolted me because it was about to happen. I was going to be fucked in the most glorious way by Oliver Wyatt. I watched as he slid the condom over his cock and then plunged his finger inside of me, feeling how wet I was because of him.

"You're so wet and so fucking delicious."

He pushed inside of me, slowly at first so he wouldn't hurt me. I'd never had anyone as big as him and I was a little nervous. Soon my nerves were calmed by the intense pleasure he gave me as he thrust in and out of me at a rapid pace. He leaned down and his lips brushed against mine.

"You feel so good," he moaned.

"So do you."

Another orgasm was brewing. He could tell and told me to stare into his eyes while I came. My body tightened and began to shake as I placed my hands on his face and looked into his eyes while the orgasm took over.

"That's it, baby. That's it! God, Delilah," he moaned as his thrusting slowed and he buried himself deep inside me, giving in to his own orgasm.

He collapsed on top of me and I could feel his pounding heart against my chest as his fingers tangled in my hair. We lay there for a moment in silence and let our rapid breathing return to normal. He kissed my lips before climbing off of me and going into the bathroom. After disposing of the condom, he walked over and sat on the edge of the bed, stroking my hair.

"That was amazing." He smiled.

"Indeed it was."

"You better go to your room."

Was he serious? He didn't want me staying the night in his bed? Fuck me and kick me out? I wanted him to hold me and I wanted to fall asleep in his warm arms. I couldn't let on how deeply hurt I felt, so I got up and slipped into my dress. He walked over to where I was standing as I bent down and grabbed my shoes.

"We can't let this change things. I'm still your employer and you're my employee."

"Are you mad that I punched Laurel?"

He softly laughed. "No. A little shocked, but not mad. Now go to bed. I'll see you in the morning." He kissed my forehead.

I walked out of his room feeling used and with tears in my eyes. At least with the other guys I'd slept with, they always wanted me to stay with them afterwards, even if they were total douchebags. I put on my nightshirt and went into the bathroom to take off my makeup. As I looked at myself in the mirror, I had a glow about me, but also a deep sadness in my eyes. Sex with Oliver was the best sex I'd ever had in my life and something that wouldn't be so easily forgotten.

The next morning, I climbed out of bed at the crack of dawn. I quietly walked down to the kitchen and was startled when I saw Oliver leaning up against the counter, waiting for a pot of coffee to finish brewing.

"Oh. I didn't know you were up already."

"Good morning. Why are you up so early?"

"Not tired anymore, I guess."

I couldn't help but stare at him in his black pajama bottoms and no shirt on. He had the most amazing body. His ripped six-pack, rock solid chest, and well-defined muscular arms aroused me more than I cared to admit.

"The coffee will be done in a minute."

"Great. I definitely need some."

Things now felt awkward after last night and I knew this would happen. I never should have slept with him, but damn, it was good. The coffee was brewed and Oliver poured me a cup and handed it to me.

"Thank you." I began to walk up the stairs.

"Where are you going?"

"Back to my room." I turned and looked at him.

"I was going to sit on the patio and drink my coffee. You don't want to join me?"

The confusion spinning around my brain was too much this early in the morning. "No. I'm going back up to my room. Enjoy your coffee." I gave him a small smile and walked up the stairs.

Strength was all I had. There was never time to be weak in my life. Too many people had depended on me over the years and I always needed to keep strong for them. If I became weak, all would fall apart and I couldn't let that happen. It was the same with Oliver. He depended on me to take care of Sophie and I needed to be strong for her sake, regardless of what a pompous ass her father was.

Chapter 22

I took a shower and got dressed before Sophie woke up. I wanted to be ready for her in case there was some last minute packing that needed to be done. As I left my room, I walked to hers and carefully opened the door. She was up and painting at her easel.

"Good morning, Soph."

"Good morning."

"What are you doing?"

"Finishing up this painting before I leave to go visit Aunt Kelsey."

I walked over to the easel and stared at the picture that sat before me. It was of a woman standing in a garden of flowers.

"Who is that?" I asked.

"My mom. This is her in Heaven." She smiled.

My heart ached at that moment as I stared at the painting. "My mom is in Heaven too."

"Maybe she knows my mom," Sophie spoke as she dipped the paintbrush in some paint.

"Maybe she does." I kissed the top of her head.

"If you have a picture of your mom, I can paint her in Heaven just like my mom."

I softly smiled as I stroked her long, blonde hair. "I would like that. Maybe when you get back from your trip."

"Okay."

I grabbed her suitcase from the corner of the room and set it on her bed. As I unzipped it, Oliver walked into the room.

"Good morning, princess. Are you almost ready to leave?"

"Hi, Daddy. Look. I'm painting a picture of Mommy."

"I see that. It's very pretty."

I looked up and Oliver glanced over at me. I double-checked to make sure Sophie had everything and then zipped up her suitcase. Oliver walked over and took it from me. Our fingers touched and flashes of last night flooded my mind, sending my body into an aroused state. I quickly moved back.

"Sophie, are you bringing your paints?" I asked to escape the awkward moment.

"No. I changed my mind. I don't think I'll have time to paint."

"Let's go, princess. I'll have Clara wash your paintbrushes."

"Okay." She smiled.

The Escalade Oliver rented was parked at the curb. He set Sophie's suitcase in the back and we all climbed in. He looked over at me in confusion as he looked at the nylon zipper bag I threw on the floor.

"What's in the bag?"

"Just a few necessities one might need in case something happens."

"Like?"

"Toothbrush, toothpaste, deodorant, a change of clothes, hairbrush, etc."

His eyes narrowed as he cocked his head at me. "You really brought all that?"

"Yeah. It's always good to be prepared just in case. You never know what could happen."

"If you say so." He gave a small smile and pulled away.

Oliver

Even though Delilah explained to me why she packed a bag, I still didn't understand why she did it. To be honest, I thought it was a little strange, but to each his own. As we drove down the highway, Delilah kept Sophie entertained by singing songs. It was a good distraction because things felt off since we had sex last night. My phone was sitting in the cup holder, and when it went off, Delilah looked at it. Laurel was calling.

"Aren't you going to answer that?" she asked.

"No."

"Want me to answer it?" She smiled.

"Are you nuts? No way."

She turned her head and looked out the window. Sophie said she needed to use the bathroom, so we pulled over and stopped at a rest area.

"I'll wait here for you. I have a phone call to make," I told Delilah.

She grabbed Sophie's hand and went to the bathroom while I called Laurel back.

"What do you want, Laurel?"

"I don't want things to end. I love you and I want us to work this out," she pleaded.

"There's nothing to work out. We're over. I'm sorry, Laurel."

"You're sorry? Well, I'll have you know that I'm pressing charges against Delilah for assault and battery."

"I don't think that's a wise idea. You may want to reconsider it."

"Too bad, Oliver. I'm doing it. So tell your nanny she'd better be prepared to deal with the consequences."

I sighed. "Laurel, I'm going to make you a deal. You are to forget about Delilah and what she did to you and maybe a certain story won't be leaked regarding you and a certain Senator a couple of years ago."

"Oliver, you wouldn't."

"Force my hand, Laurel, and see what happens. You are to stay away from my nanny. You aren't even allowed to say her name. Do you understand me? If you hurt Delilah, then you hurt Sophie and I won't let anyone, including you, hurt my daughter. The consequences for you if that story gets out will be far worse than the consequences for Delilah would be."

"I hope you both rot in Hell." *Click.*

I couldn't help but let out a small smile as I placed my phone in my pocket. Delilah and Sophie climbed back in the Escalade and we continued our journey to Vermont. The ride was silent. Sophie fell asleep in the back seat and Delilah had her earphones in, looking out the passenger window. I kept looking over at her. It was taking everything I had not to run the back of my hand down her cheek. To feel her soft skin like I did last night.

****

Delilah

I pressed pause on my iPod and took out my earphones as I looked over at Sophie sleeping.

"How much longer?" I asked.

"About an hour."

I couldn't stop staring at him. The way he had his seat leaned back with his right hand gripped at the top of the leather steering wheel was so sexy. I was still mad at him for last night, but I was relieved that he broke up with Laurel.

"Did you call Laurel back?" I asked, expecting him to tell me it was none of my business.

He glanced over at me for a second before answering. "Yes. But if you don't mind, I don't want to talk about it."

"That's fine. I'm sure she'll be pressing charges against me for punching her."

"No she won't. You don't have to worry about that."

"She seems like a very vindictive person. So I expect it."

"Trust me, Delilah. She's not pressing charges. She was going to until I threatened to expose a little secret of hers."

"Oh. What kind of secret? I'm sure you won't tell me anyway."

"No. I won't tell you, but it is one that will get her and a very influential person in a lot of trouble."

It made me happy that he stuck up for me. "Thank you for defending me." I smiled.

"No problem. I can't have her pressing charges against my daughter's nanny. Imagine what that would do to Sophie."

I gave him a small smile as I heard Sophie stirring in the backseat. "Hey, sunshine. Did you have a nice nap?"

"Yeah. Are we almost there?" she asked.

"One more hour, princess," Oliver replied.

"Can we listen to some music, Delilah?"

"Sure we can. Let's see what's on the radio."

I was flipping through the radio stations and the beginning of "Midnight Train to Georgia" started to play.

"Oh. I love this song. Do you know it, Oliver?"

"Yes." He smiled as he looked at me.

"Great. We can sing together."

"No, Delilah. I don't sing."

"Daddy. Please sing with Delilah," Sophie whined. "Please, Daddy."

"Okay. Okay." He laughed.

I began to sing and dance in my seat as I pointed to Oliver when it was his turn. He was enjoying it. In fact, this was the first time since I'd known him that I saw him having some fun. Sophie was laughing at us from the back seat. As the song ended, I placed my hand on his arm and he glanced at me with a wide smile.

"That was fun, Daddy! I like the way you sing."

"Thank you, darling. But don't get too used to it."

Chapter 23

Oliver

As soon as we pulled up to Matt and Kelsey's house, the front door opened and they walked outside. Kelsey didn't like me and I knew this was going to make for an awkward situation. She called me a heartless manwhore because of Elaine. Even though Elaine's family despised me, I did the right thing by not letting them know she had killed herself. The three of us got out of the car and Sophie ran up to Kelsey, giving her a big hug.

"God, I've missed you. Look at how you've grown. How are you, Sophie?"

"I'm good, Aunt Kelsey."

Matt looked at me and extended his hand. "Hello, Oliver."

I lightly shook it. "Matt. How are you?"

"No complaints."

I looked over at Kelsey. "Kelsey. It's good to see you."

"Oliver. Thanks for letting Sophie come and stay with us."

"You're welcome. I would like you to meet Delilah, Sophie's nanny."

She gave Delilah a warm smile and held out her hand. "It's nice to meet you, Delilah."

"Likewise."

"Can I see the animals?!" Sophie exclaimed.

"Of course you can." Matt took her by the hand. I followed them while Kelsey invited Delilah inside for some lemonade.

****

Delilah

Kelsey handed me a glass of lemonade and we walked out to the back and took a seat at the picnic table while Matt, Oliver, and Sophie looked at the horses.

"How has Sophie been?" Kelsey asked.

"She's been great. She's really smart. You should see how she paints."

"How is she adjusting to living with Oliver?"

"She's good. I've been spending a great deal of time with her."

"Isn't her father supposed to be doing that?"

I sighed as I stared at Oliver from a distance. "He told me that you don't like him."

"He's right. I don't. In fact, I can't stand him. All Elaine wanted was a family and he led her on, making her believe that he loved her until she got pregnant, then he kicked her to the curb and refused to have anything to do with Sophie. Elaine dies and all of a sudden he steps up and wants to play daddy? He's no good for her. She would do better if Matt and I were to raise her."

"He's her father." I started to become angry.

"I know that, but it doesn't make him a better parent."

"Oliver is doing the best he can. He loves that little girl more than life."

"The only thing he can do for her is provide her with material things."

I took a sip of lemonade and before I could comment, Sophie ran over to me.

"Delilah, I got to pet the horse and Uncle Matt said that he'll teach me how to ride."

"That's great, baby." I pulled her into me.

183

Matt and Oliver walked over to where we were sitting. "Delilah, are you ready to head back? We have a long ride ahead of us."

"Yeah." I got up from my seat and gave Sophie a hug goodbye. "You're going to have so much fun here. Be good and when you get home, I'll take you to the museum."

Oliver bent down and hugged her tight, kissing her on the head. "I'll miss you, princess. Be good for your Aunt Kelsey and Uncle Matt. Remember, you can call me at any time. I love you, Sophie."

"I love you too, Daddy."

We said goodbye to Kelsey and Matt and climbed in the Escalade. I could tell that Oliver was somewhat off. Perhaps he was sad that Sophie wasn't going back with us. He pulled out of the driveway and we headed on our journey back to New York.

"You okay?" I asked as I looked over at him.

"Yeah. I just didn't think I'd be missing my daughter already."

"It's hard. I remember when Braden first went off to college. It was so weird not having him around. I felt empty inside."

He looked at me with a small smile and reached over and squeezed my hand. "This will be good for Sophie. She should spend some time with her mother's family. I wanted to wait until we were alone to talk about last night."

"What about it?" I asked.

"I got the impression you're pissed off at me for some reason and I would like to know why."

I cocked my head as I looked at him and narrowed my eyes. If he truly didn't know, then he would have to keep guessing because I wasn't about to have this discussion with him.

"Why would you get that impression?"

"Well, for starters, you wouldn't have coffee with me this morning. Do you regret what happened between us?"

"Do you?" I asked.

He didn't say anything as he looked straight ahead. "Listen, Oliver. You had just broken up with Laurel and you were in a vulnerable state. It happens. Sometimes a person seeks sex to make themselves feel better. I was there and we had sex. It's not like it meant anything. It was a release for your pain and/or loss. To be blunt, it was just sex. So get over yourself and stop thinking I'm mad."

"That was a little brutal, Delilah. Don't you think?"

"No. You asked me a question and I gave you my honest answer."

He needed me to tell him I wasn't mad, so I did. I did it for the sake of our professional relationship as well as friendship. Did I believe that line of bullshit I just fed him? No. The truth was, it was more than just sex for me. I wished I had a switch that I could just flip and say no big deal. But I didn't and, to me, it was on a whole new personal level. But I needed him to believe that all was good.

We were about two and a half hours into our drive and I suspected that Oliver got on the wrong highway because we had just entered Rockport, Massachusetts.

"I think you're going the wrong way."

"I know where I'm going. It's the same route we took to Vermont."

"Really? Why don't you use the GPS and find out? Because I don't remember going through Rockport."

"Delilah, don't be a back seat driver."

I pulled out my phone and pulled up the GPS. I typed in our location and Manhattan, New York.

"Yep. You went the wrong way. It says here that Manhattan is four hours and sixteen minutes from here."

"Impossible. Let me see that." He took the phone from my hand and the Escalade started to shake. "Shit!" Oliver yelled.

"What's wrong? Why is the car doing that shaky thing?"

"I don't know. I need to pull over." He sighed as he pulled over on the side of the road and the Escalade shut down. He tried to start it again and it was completely dead.

"You have got to be fucking kidding me." He got out and slammed the door.

I climbed out and walked around to where he was leaned up against the truck, pulling his phone from his pocket.

"Who are you calling?"

"The car rental place."

Up ahead was a restaurant called Ellen's Diner. I grabbed my purse and bag and began walking towards it.

"Where are you going?" he yelled.

"I'm hungry and there's a diner up ahead."

He ran and caught up to me. "How can you think about food right now? The rental place is closed and we're stuck here."

"That might be, but it doesn't change the fact that I'm starving. Let's grab some dinner and figure out what to do next."

He sighed and I silently smiled. We reached the diner and walked inside. The place was jammed packed, but there was one open booth in the corner. I grabbed two menus that sat behind the napkin holder and handed one to Oliver. He took it from me and gave me an unpleasant look.

"What was that look for?"

"I don't understand how you can eat at a time like this."

I laughed. "Time like what? You mean because the rental car broke down?"

"Yes."

"It's a minor thing. We'll eventually make it back to New York." I smiled.

The waitress walked over and Oliver asked her if there was a rental car place nearby. She replied as she annoyingly chewed on her gum.

"There's a place about twenty miles from here, but it's closed now. They'll reopen tomorrow at nine a.m."

He looked irritated and I ordered a coke.

"Now what are we supposed to do?" he asked me.

"How do I know? You're the man. Shouldn't you know these things?"

"I'll call Scott."

"Really? So you want to sit here for the next four hours for Scott and then drive four hours home? Does that make sense?"

"Then it looks like we'll have to spend the night in Rockport," he replied.

"Good thing I packed a bag." I smiled as I held it up. "And you thought it was a stupid idea."

"I never said it was stupid." He winked.

When the waitress delivered our dinner, Oliver asked her where the nearest hotel was.

"Right down the road is the Yankee Clipper Inn, but good luck because it's prime tourist season right now and all the hotels are pretty booked up."

"Great." He scowled as he looked at me. "Thank you. We'll try there."

He pulled out his phone and looked the number up, calling them to inquire about rooms. "If that's all you have, then I'll take it. We'll be checking in shortly."

As I was indulging in my cheeseburger, he hung up and placed his phone back in his pocket.

"So they have rooms available?"

"Yes, but only one. The people had to check out early due to a family emergency."

"But we need two rooms." My stomach started to flutter at the thought of staying in the same room with him.

"They don't have two rooms. Only one. We don't have a choice."

"We wouldn't be in this situation if you would have used the GPS to go home."

"The car still would have broken down." He narrowed his eyes at me.

"Yes, but we would have been closer to home."

He sighed. "Finish your dinner so we can get out of here."

I gave him a cocky smile as I took a bite of my French fry.

Chapter 24

Oliver

I took Delilah's bag from her as we left the diner and headed down the road to the Yankee Clipper Inn. I had to admit that Rockport was a beautiful place.

"It's pretty here," I said as I threw her bag over my shoulder.

"I was just thinking that too."

As mad as I was that the Escalade had broken down and we were stuck here, I loved the fact that it happened with Delilah. I wanted to fuck her again more than anything else in the world. She was incredible last night and left me craving her even more than I already had been. I hoped she'd be open to having sex again tonight because being in the same room with her wasn't going to be easy. My feelings had escalated beyond my wildest dreams and it terrified me. When we reached the driveway to the Inn, we stopped in front of it and looked up. The beautiful

1920s-style white mansion sat far back and on a small hill near the ocean.

"Are you ready to climb this hill, Mr. Wyatt?" Delilah smiled at me.

"I am if you are." I smiled back and held out my hand. She took it and every nerve in my body jolted.

We walked inside and took note of the Victorian style décor that graced the interior of the place.

"Wow. This is beautiful, Oliver."

I walked up to the desk and gave the man, whose name tag said "Bob," my name.

"You will be in room number six on the third floor, Mr. Wyatt."

"Thank you." I graciously smiled as he handed me a gold key.

We walked up the stairs and I inserted the key into the lock. It was your standard doorknob with a regular lock. When we walked inside, Delilah went right over to the door wall and opened the sliding door.

"Oh my God, look at this view and listen to that ocean."

I set her bag on the bed and walked over to where she was standing on the balcony. It was a beautiful sight.

"Haven't you ever seen the ocean before?"

"Ha. You're kidding me, right? You knew how and where I grew up. The only thing I ever saw were alleyways, garbage cans, and drug dealers hanging on the street corners. I need to go down there and feel the water," she said in excitement as she flew out the door.

"Delilah, wait!"

I ran after her. There was no sand. It was all rocks and I didn't want her to fall. Once she saw the rocks, she stopped.

"Take my hand and I'll help you down there."

She put her in hand in mine and I carefully led her over the rocks and down to the water. She bent down and looked up at me with a smile as she moved her hands around lightly in the water. Watching the excitement on her face was overwhelming. Something that I took for granted and had seen a million times was so new and refreshing to her. I bent down beside her and placed my hands in the water as she turned and looked at me.

"Thank you for helping me down here."

"It was my pleasure, Miss Graham." Against my better judgment, I leaned in and softly brushed my lips against hers. I needed to feel her lips on mine once again.

****

Delilah

He caught me off guard with his kiss, but I didn't care. I was happy to finally see the ocean and feel the saltwater, even if it was by accident because the Escalade had broken down. His kiss was soft but unsure. Unsure if he should have touched my lips. There was no doubt that I was falling more and more for him every day. I placed my hand on his cheek and smiled. He smiled back and took my hand, helping me up amongst the rocks as we walked back to the Inn. When we reached the room, my heart began to race as he placed his hands on my hips and stared into my eyes.

"May I kiss you again?" he asked.

"Why are you asking? You didn't ask before."

The corners of his mouth curled up into that sweet smile that I'd grown to love. "I'll take that as a yes, then." He leaned closer, and as his lips touched mine with force, I trembled. His kiss was untamed as his hands moved up and down my body. The feel of his tongue against mine sent shivers throughout my body and the excitement and longing for him brewed down below. I wasn't stopping him, even though I should have after what had happened last night. His fingers gripped the bottom of my shirt as he broke our kiss and lifted it over my head. My hands fearlessly grabbed at his belt and as soon as I unbuckled it, I went for his button. He moaned as his tongue slid up and around my neck, caressing the edge of my ear and sending my body into overdrive. Unzipping his zipper, I slid my hand down the front of his pants, grasping his hard, beautiful cock, which had given me so much pleasure.

"God, Delilah," he whispered as his mouth kissed its way down to the center of my breasts. He reached behind and unhooked my bra, tossing it across the room while he took my hardened nipple in his mouth. It wasn't long before his hands unbuttoned my shorts and took them down along with my panties. The palm of his hand pushed against me as his thumb circled my clit. My breathing was rapid as several moans escaped me and he dipped his fingers inside.

"You're so wet. Fuck. I need to taste you."

He pushed me back on the bed and spread my legs as his mouth devoured me, his tongue flickering against my clit, causing me to climax. I grasped the bed comforter as I released myself. He smiled as he softly kissed the inside of my thighs before trailing up my torso and reaching my breasts, lightly taking them between his teeth and then licking to cool the sting. God, I was in Heaven and I never wanted him to stop.

"I want that sweet mouth of yours wrapped around my cock." He stood up at the edge of the bed as I sat up and got on my knees in front of him and wrapped my lips around him, taking his manhood in my mouth. His moans became louder as I sucked up and down his shaft and swirled my tongue around, sending him into a frenzy after I started caressing his balls. His fingers tangled in my hair as he moved my head up and down.

"Shit, Delilah. Your mouth is amazing. I'm going to come any second. Watching you blow me is so fucking hot. Oh my God," he moaned as he pulled out of my mouth and came all over my breasts. He took my face in his hands and I lay on my back. He hovered over me and softly kissed me.

"We should clean you up." He smiled and walked to the bathroom and grabbed some tissue.

He climbed on the bed next to me and cleaned his come from my breasts, smiling as he was doing it.

"That was nice. Thank you. But I still need to be inside of you."

"What are you waiting for?" I asked with a grin.

He threw the tissue on the nightstand and grabbed his wallet, which was sitting there. He pulled out the condom and set it down.

****

Oliver

She looked like nothing except a goddess lying on the bed naked in front of me. I ran my finger around her lips and she took it in her mouth, sucking it as she stared at me. My cock was rising faster than the speed of light and aching to be inside of her. Pulling my finger from her mouth, I traced around her beautiful breasts, circling her already hardened nipples before making my way down to her tight pussy. She moaned as I dipped my finger inside of her, slowly feeling my way around inside. Feeling the warmth of the wetness that emerged from her delighted me in ways that were unexplainable. She excited me more than any other woman ever had and the way I lusted for her was insane. I wanted to make love to her, not fuck her any which way like an animal. I wanted to move slowly in and out of her, savoring each and every pleasurable stroke. My cock was hard and ready to explode. I reached over to the nightstand, ripped open the condom wrapper, and slid it over me. Rolling her on her side, I lay next to her, wrapping my arms around her and groping her perfect breasts as I slowly entered her. She gasped and I let out a soft moan. As I moved fluidly in and out of her, our bodies began to sweat. I lightly circled her shoulder with my tongue as my finger found her clit. It drove her wild as she turned her head and smashed her mouth against mine. She had me so hot I couldn't hold back any more. As the orgasm consumed her body, I pushed myself deep inside her as I took pleasure in my release.

Chapter 25

Delilah

God, my body was on fire. Still reeling from the effects of what Oliver did to me, I lay there as he pulled out and got up to dispose of the condom. I climbed under the covers with a knot in my stomach for what was to come next. Oliver walked from the bathroom and started to climb in next to me.

"What are you doing?"

"Getting in bed?" he spoke with confusion.

"Not in this bed, you're not."

"Excuse me?" He arched his eyebrow.

I took the extra pillow from the bed and threw it on the floor. "You can sleep on the floor or in that chair over there."

"What's going on here?"

"I wasn't good enough to sleep next to last night, but tonight is different? Why? Because you can't send me to my room?"

"That's why you were pissed," he said as he sat down on the bed.

"Damn right, I was pissed, Oliver. I felt like a hooker. 'Thanks for the fuck, now get out of here.'"

He sighed. "Delilah, listen to me. The only reason I did that was because of Sophie. I didn't want her to find us together in bed. That wouldn't be right."

Okay. Now I felt like a complete ass. But it was his fault for not explaining that to me.

"I'm sorry. I should have told you that last night, and to be honest, I didn't think about it and I seriously didn't think you'd be mad about it."

"I was more hurt, Oliver," I spoke as I turned the other way.

"I wanted you to stay in my bed. I wanted to wrap my arms around you and fall asleep with your naked body against mine after the amazing sex we had, but I couldn't risk it. What if she would have gotten up in the middle of the night and come to either one of our rooms?"

His words made me melt and, instantly, he was forgiven because he made a valid point. "You're right and I'm sorry. Now get under these covers and hold me."

He picked the pillow up off the floor and climbed in, wrapping his strong arms around me and pulling me tight against his chest. He was so warm and my body was heating up with desire.

"It would be my pleasure to hold you all night long."

I smiled as I kissed his chest. This man, my boss, my friend, was making me feel like the most special person in the world. I wouldn't take this happiness I felt for granted because I knew it wasn't going to last. Nothing lasts forever.

****

I awoke to the sound of my and Oliver's phone buzzing. I reached over and grabbed mine, as did Oliver. I had a text message from Liam.

"Where are you and Oliver? I thought you were coming back yesterday?"

"It's Liam. Didn't you call him or text him last night?" I asked Oliver.

"I forgot. I had something else on my mind." He kissed the top of my head.

"The Escalade broke down and we had to spend the night in Rockport, MA. Oliver will explain."

"Whoa. Are you two in the same room?"

"Yes."

"It's about damn time."

I smiled and Oliver decided to call him. I got out of bed and headed to the bathroom. When I returned, Oliver had just hung up with Liam.

"I have to call the rental place now."

I climbed back into bed and on top of him, kissing his soft lips. "I think that can wait for now." I smiled.

"As much as I would love to, Delilah, I'm afraid that was the only condom I had."

"Oh. Well, you don't have to worry about that. I'm on the pill. I have been for the past three years."

"You haven't been having sex. Why are you on birth control?"

"I used to get horrible cramps around that time of the month. Cramps so debilitating that I couldn't get out of bed. The pill helps that."

"Ah. I see. Well, I don't feel safe without using a condom. So if there's no condom, there's no sex. I made that mistake once and I won't make it again."

I looked at him with a frown and climbed off of him. *There goes my happy.* I knew it wouldn't last. He basically said he didn't trust me and that hurt. In fact, it hurt more than it should have.

"Okay, then. Make your phone call. I'm going to take a shower." I got up, went into the bathroom, and locked the door.

After my shower, Oliver was dressed and sitting out on the balcony. "Do you want to take one last look at the ocean before we leave?"

"No. I got my fix last night. I'm good. What did the rental place say?"

"They're coming to tow the Escalade and bringing out another car for us. They'll be here in about an hour, so why don't we go downstairs and have breakfast first?"

"Okay." I threw my stuff back in my bag, grabbed my purse, and headed out the door. Oliver followed behind and I made sure I stayed ahead of him.

"Why are you walking so fast?"

"I'm hungry," I lied.

We reached the dining area and took a seat at a table for two. While waiting for our breakfast, I sipped my coffee while Oliver played on his phone. These next couple of weeks without

Sophie being around were going to be strange. I was going to make sure I was busy so I didn't have to think about him too much.

"I think I'll give Kelsey a call and talk to Sophie to see how she's doing."

"Good idea." I pulled my phone from my purse and there was a text message from Jenny.

"How did the trip to Vermont go?"

"The rental car broke down in Rockport, MA on the way back and we had to stay the night."

"Together? Same room? For the love of God, please say yes."

I smiled as I read her message. *"Yes. It was amazing and I have no words. I'll tell you all about it when I get back. Dinner tonight?"*

"Yes. Come to the apartment. I'll make Stephen cook for us."

"Sounds good. I'll see you later."

"Can't wait to hear all the juicy details."

Oliver talked to Sophie and then handed me his phone. "Sophie would like to talk to you."

I gave a small smile as I brought the phone up to my ear.

"Hello, sunshine. Are you having fun?"

"Hi, Delilah. I got to ride a horse and feed the goats and the chickens."

"That's great, Soph. I'm so happy for you."

"I have to go. Aunt Kelsey is going to show me how to milk the cows."

"You have fun with that. We'll talk soon."

"I love you, Delilah," her sweet little voice spoke.

"I love you too, baby."

I handed the phone to Oliver and, after eating breakfast, we walked back to where the Escalade broke down. The tow truck had just arrived and so had our rental car. I climbed in the passenger seat of the Jeep Cherokee as Oliver signed some papers. This was a beautiful town and I wished I could have seen more of it.

"Ready to head home?" he asked as he climbed in and fastened his seat belt.

"Yep."

As we were driving down the highway, and the right one this time, I decided to make conversation with Oliver about Laurel. I wanted to know more about her and their relationship.

"How long had you and Laurel dated?" I asked.

He looked over at me with surprise. "Why?"

"Just trying to make conversation."

"Eight months." He kept his eyes focused on the road. "I remember you telling me that the longest relationship you had was a few days because there wasn't time for guys. But, if you had met the right guy, you would have dated him longer than a few days. Right?"

"Nah. Relationships are toxic to the soul."

He glanced over at me and gave a small smile. "You think so?"

"It's what my mom always used to tell me. She said that relationships change people and, soon enough, after the thrill was over, and you give yourself and your heart to another person, toxicity would set in and, eventually, you become miserable and stop being who you were meant to be."

"That's pretty deep. But wasn't she drunk more than half the time?"

"She was drunk all of the time. Not just half. I never saw her without a drink in her hand. You know how some people wake up and the first thing they do is pour a cup of coffee?"

"Yeah."

"Well, she would wake up and pour herself a glass of vodka."

"I'm sorry you had to live like that," he spoke with sincerity.

"I did what I had to do to take care of her and my brothers and sister. I'm sorry to say this, but you never looked happy when you were with Laurel."

He sighed. "I guess I wasn't. It really showed, eh?"

"Yep."

"Then I guess she was toxic." He winked.

Finally, we were home and as we entered the house, Liam came walking from the kitchen.

"Well, well, well, look at what the sunshine brought home." He smiled as he kissed my cheek. "Good to see you both are safe."

"Thanks, Liam," Oliver spoke and rolled his eyes. "What are you doing here?"

"I just dropped off some papers you need to look over. I didn't know if you'd be coming to the office today and you need to review them and sign them by tomorrow."

"I'll look at them after I shower." He walked up the stairs and I went to the kitchen for a bottle of water. Liam followed behind.

"So. You and Oliver?" He grinned.

"No. There is no me and Oliver and, for god sakes, he just broke up with Laurel."

"I know. Isn't it exciting? It's about damn time he dumped that trash bag. So are you claiming you didn't have sex with him?"

"Did I say that?"

"Answering a question with a question, which means you did. Congratulations."

I narrowed my eyes at him. "Thank you? Now, if you'll excuse me, I'm going to run upstairs and change my clothes."

"Delilah, wait."

I stopped on the stairs and looked at him.

"Be careful where Oliver is concerned. I don't want you getting hurt."

"I can handle Oliver." I winked and went upstairs.

Chapter 26

Oliver

After my shower, I walked over to the bar and poured myself a glass of scotch. Liam walked in with a smile on his face.

"Drink?" I asked.

"Sure."

"What's the smile for?" I handed him his glass and walked to my office.

"Nothing special. Glad you're home. Sorry about you and Laurel." He took a seat across from my desk.

"Yeah. I'm sure you are."

"Okay. I'm not. I actually celebrated the good news. Too bad you weren't here to celebrate with me. But wait, I do believe you were celebrating with a girl named Delilah." He flashed his cocky smile.

"Why do you say that? Just because we shared the same room doesn't mean we shared a bed together."

"Right. If you think I believe that, then you must think I'm stupid, which I know damn well you don't. So. Spill it. How was it?"

"Amazing. Best sex I'd ever had."

"Whoa. That's a lot coming from you."

"Now I don't want to discuss it again. I spoke with Laurel yesterday. She told me she was going to press assault and battery charges against Delilah. I'd advised her not to or else a certain story would surface."

The grin on his face grew wide and he slowly nodded his head. "Very good. I'm assuming she changed her mind?"

"Of course she did. Immediately."

The smell of lavender filtered through the room as I looked up and saw Delilah standing in the doorway.

"Sorry to interrupt, but I wanted you to know that I'm heading out."

"Heading out? I thought we'd have dinner together."

"Sorry, boss, but I'm having dinner with Stephen and Jenny over at their apartment. I'll be home later tonight." She flashed a smile as she turned around.

"Wait. Are you having Scott drive you?"

"No. I can cab it. I'm a big girl."

She left, and suddenly, a feeling washed over me that I couldn't explain.

"Boss? Does she always call you that?"

"No. That was the first time. I can't fucking believe she left." I got up from my chair and walked out of my office and over to the bar for another drink.

"She's having dinner with her best friend. Wait a minute. You are really pissed off. Did you ask her to have dinner with you or did you just assume she would?"

I sighed as I took a drink. "I figured we'd be here together tonight and we'd have dinner. She didn't tell me she had plans."

"Why does she need to tell you? Sophie isn't here, so she's free to do whatever she wants. Maybe if you would have asked her earlier, things would be different."

"Liam, don't you have something to do?"

"Yeah. Actually, I do. I'm having dinner with my big brother tonight. So come on; we'll go grab a burger and a couple of beers."

"Fine. But there will be no talk of Delilah or any questions asked. Understand?"

"Yes, boss." He smiled.

****

Delilah

I walked into my old apartment and it still felt like home. The smell of roasted chicken and vegetables filled the small space. I looked around and didn't see Jenny or Stephen. I had a feeling they were probably having sex.

"I'm home!" I yelled.

Jenny squealed as she came running from the bedroom while putting on her shirt. "I'm so happy you're here."

"I didn't interrupt anything, did I?"

"Nah. We had just finished. I want to hear all about your fucktastical day yesterday and how yummy Oliver was."

"Do you have a bottle of wine?"

"Of course. Already opened and waiting."

Stephen emerged with a bright smile on his face. "Hey, Delilah. Good to see you, babe." He leaned over and kissed my cheek.

"Good to see you too, Stephen."

"You ladies go sit down and I will bring dinner to you. I'm sure you have a lot of girly talk to do since Jenny wouldn't stop talking about it yesterday."

Jenny grabbed the bottle of wine from the counter and we sat down at the table.

"So." She smiled as she tilted the bottle to my glass.

"Yesterday wasn't the first time. I slept with him the night of the fundraiser."

"WHAT? And you didn't call me!"

"Everything happened so fast. First of all, I ended up decking Laurel in the face after she called me a whore."

"Shut up! You did not." Her face screamed with excitement.

"Yes, I did. It wasn't one of my finer moments, but she had pushed me over the edge."

"Kind of like that Sammy chick back in high school. Remember her?"

I rolled my eyes. "Don't remind me. Anyway, Oliver broke up with Laurel after that and came home. I was in the kitchen putting ice on my hand when he walked in and, I guess you could say, took care of me."

"So romantic." She swooned.

Stephen set dinner on the table and sat down next to Jenny. We ate, drank, and talked some more about Oliver.

"You've fallen for him. I can tell. Of all the years I've known you, you have never been about a guy like this."

She was right. I'd never met anyone I truly cared about, but with Oliver, it just seemed natural. There was something about him that excited me. Something that aroused me in places I never thought possible. Maybe it was the fact that he was older and mature. All I knew was that I was head over heels for him. For the first time in my life, I was in love and I was scared.

****

I opened the door and went to the kitchen to grab a bottle of water to take upstairs. When I closed the refrigerator, Oliver walked in.

"Hey. Did you just get in?" I asked.

"Yeah. I went to dinner with Liam. How was your evening?"

"It was fun. It was good to catch up with Jenny and Stephen."

He stood there and stared at me for a moment. He had that desire in his eyes that I'd come to notice. He slowly walked over to where I was standing and ran his finger across my lips.

"Have you ever been fucked on the kitchen counter?"

"No." I gulped.

"Would you like to be?" His finger traveled down the front of my dress.

"Yes." I swallowed hard.

"Good. Because I want to fuck you right now and right here." He took down the straps of my sundress and let it fall to the ground. His hands latched onto both of my breasts as he kneaded them through the fabric of my bra. Gazing into my eyes, his hands moved down and his fingers gripped the sides of my panties, pulling them all the way down and then cupping me with his hand.

"You're so wet already and I haven't even been down there yet to taste you." He smiled. "Do I excite you, Delilah?"

"Yes." I panted as he dipped his fingers inside me.

"Do you like it when I play with you like this?" His fingers moved in and out of me slowly.

"Very much."

My body was pulsating and fire had erupted across my skin. He reached up with his other hand and undid my bra, throwing it on the floor while my hand instinctively traveled to the bulge in his pants. He softly pressed on my clit, stroking it up and down and sending me into a frenzy. This man knew exactly how to please a woman. He pulled his fingers out and lifted me up on the counter. After lifting his shirt over his head and then taking down his pants, he pushed me back and lifted my legs over his shoulder as he tasted me, sucking and lapping up the pool of wetness he caused. I leaned back in total euphoria and moaned like I'd never moaned before, while my body prepared for an amazing orgasm. His hands reached up and his fingers latched onto my hardened nipples, tugging and rubbing them with seductive pleasure.

"Before I stick my cock in you, you need to come for me. You need to show me how much you love what I do to you."

His words, his mouth, his hands sent me over the cliff as I nosedived into the pure bliss of an orgasm. I let out a loud moan with his name and I could feel his smile down below as I released myself. He stood up, releasing my legs, and smashed his mouth into mine, making me taste what he had done to me.

"I've never been so turned on as I am with you," he spoke with bated breath.

He broke our passionate kiss and tore open the condom that he retrieved from his wallet. After slipping it over his hard cock, he pulled me to the edge of the counter, sucking my nipples before thrusting inside of me. I gasped as he moved in and out of me at a rapid pace. Our lips twisted and our tongues tangled. While he was deep inside of me, he pulled me off the counter and carried me over to the wall beside the staircase, where he continued to thrust in and out of me as he held me up, gripping my ass as tight as he could.

His strength was amazing and I felt safe tangled around his body. I held his face in my hands as I stared into his eyes and watched his lips part with soft moans. It hit me at that moment that I was officially in love with him. I threw my head back as my body shook and he pushed one last time inside of me as we came in sync. He buried his face into my neck and softly kissed my heated skin. Once our heart rates calmed, he pulled out of me and set me down. My legs felt like jelly and were steadily shaking. He removed the condom and disposed of it in the nearby trashcan. Walking back over to me, he picked me up and carried me up the stairs, kissing my lips the entire way to his bedroom. After setting me down, he pulled back the covers and we both climbed into bed. His arms wrapped tightly around me as I lay my head on his chest.

Chapter 27

I awoke to Oliver's hard cock pressed against my back. I smiled as I turned my head and he was staring at me.

"Good morning," I whispered.

He reached down and softly brushed his lips against mine.

"Good morning. I was hoping you'd take a shower with me."

"I would love to take a shower with you."

I'd never had shower sex and the thought excited me. Suddenly, something occurred to me.

"Oh my God, Oliver, we never picked up our clothes off the kitchen floor. Clara is probably downstairs right now, picking them up and shaking her head."

"Well, there's nothing we can do about it now. I guess when we go down there, we'll have to hide our heads in shame." He winked.

God, it was too early for him to be so sexy. We took a shower and Oliver made sure that my first time having shower sex was unforgettable. Everything he did to me was unforgettable.

"I'm going to go to my room and throw on some clothes. I'll meet you downstairs." I began to walk away and he grabbed my arm and pulled me into him.

"Not so fast. I need to feel those lips one more time." He kissed me deeply and passionately for a few moments before letting me go.

As I threw on a pair of yoga pants and a tank top, my lips trembled from his kiss. In fact, my whole body stilled trembled from the amazing sex we'd had last night and this morning. I tiptoed down the stairs and abruptly stopped when I saw Clara and Liam in the kitchen.

"Well, good morning. Did you have fun last night?" Liam smiled as he held up my bra.

"Give me that!" I walked over to him and grabbed it from his hand.

He chuckled and gave me a kiss on the cheek. "I'm going to sit down and enjoy my coffee. I'll see you in a few." I looked over at Clara as she stood in front of the stove cooking eggs.

"I had quite a mess to clean up this morning when I came in."

"Clara, I'm so sorry. I—"

"No need to explain. I knew it was bound to happen sooner or later. I could tell by the way Mr. Wyatt was acting."

"Really?"

She turned around and smiled at me. "Yes, and I'll happily pick up yours and Mr. Wyatt's clothes anytime, especially if I never have to see that wretched woman again."

"Oliver and Laurel broke up the night of the fundraiser."

"Yes. I know. Liam told me and he also said that you punched her."

I looked down. "Not one of my finer moments."

She put the eggs on a large plate and walked over to me, pulling me into an embrace. "You did good. She deserved it. Now go sit down and I'll bring your coffee and breakfast." She smiled.

"Thanks."

"You're welcome. You are a breath of fresh air in this house, Delilah, and I like having you around."

I gave her a kiss on the cheek and went into the dining room. Oliver was already sitting at the table.

"Oh. So I see you took the other stairs to avoid Clara."

"Maybe." He winked.

She walked into the dining room and set breakfast on the table. "Good morning, Mr. Wyatt." She smiled.

Oliver cleared his throat. "Good morning, Clara."

Liam started to laugh.

"I spoke with Sophie after you left the bedroom."

"How is she?"

"She's doing very well. She's enjoying her time with Kelsey and Matt. She said she misses us."

"I'm glad she's having a good time."

Oliver looked to Liam. "When do we get to meet Isabelle?" he asked.

"We aren't seeing each other anymore. She was too high maintenance. She reminded me of Laurel. Red flags started going up and I bolted."

"Aw, I'm sorry," I pouted.

"It's okay. I'm still exploring. Testing the waters." He winked.

****

Oliver

The next week and a half went by fast and I was the happiest I'd ever been. Delilah and I spent a lot of time together in the bedroom and we couldn't seem to get enough of each other. She was amazing in bed and fucked me like no other woman ever had. The feeling that crept up inside me when I was with her unnerved me. When she wasn't around, I couldn't stop thinking about her. I found myself missing her while I was at the office. Wondering what she was doing, what she was eating, who she was seeing. One day, during the middle of the afternoon, I was on my way to a meeting when I saw her sitting on the street corner, playing her guitar. I made Scott pull over and I stood at a distance and watched her. Her smile lit up all of New York and she touched the souls of people that were around her with her music. The final numbers for our fundraiser came in and we had made close to a million dollars. That was double what we made last year and I knew Delilah was responsible for part of that. People genuinely liked her when they were in her presence. She was the type of girl who deserved the world, especially after the life she had lived. I didn't know how things were going to change when Sophie returned home. We would have to be more careful than what we had been. We spent all of our nights in my bedroom, making love and enjoying each other's company. I felt like we were in some sort of fantasy world and that when Sophie came home, we'd be back to reality.

Everything was going perfectly until one night, when she said something in her sleep.

"I love you, Oliver."

When I heard her say those words, I became unhinged. Many women had spoken those three words to me before and I didn't give a damn. It never affected me and I was able to brush it off as nothing. But when Delilah said them, even though she was asleep, memories flooded my mind and I went back to when I was seventeen years old. I climbed out of bed and poured myself a drink and took a seat at the piano, softly pressing one key at a time.

"Hey. Are you okay?" I heard her angelic voice say.

"I'm fine. I just couldn't sleep. I have a lot on my mind."

She walked over to me and placed her hands on my shoulders. Her touch was just as overwhelming as always.

"Is there anything I can do?"

"No. Go back to bed," I spoke sternly.

She sensed something was wrong, but I couldn't tell her what she'd said and how I felt.

"Oliver, what's wrong?"

"I told you I have a lot on my mind. Now do as I say and go back to bed."

"Excuse me? You will not speak to me that way. When you're ready to talk, I'll be in my room, sleeping in my own bed." She walked away.

I sighed. I was changing, becoming the man I once was. I was losing control; the control I'd spent so many years building.

Chapter 28

Delilah

I lay in my own bed with tears streaming down my face. I didn't understand what happened and why Oliver would speak to me the way he did. He didn't come to my room last night and I was nervous as hell to see him this morning. I walked downstairs and grabbed some coffee.

"Good morning, Clara. Has Oliver been down yet?"

"Yes. He's gone already."

"What? Why?"

"I don't know, Delilah. He didn't say."

I took my coffee and sat outside on the patio and pondered what could have prompted Oliver's sudden change in behavior. When we fell asleep, everything was perfect. We had just had mind-blowing sex for the second time. The way he spoke to me was out of anger and I couldn't figure out for the life of me what could have happened, and I hated him at that moment for not opening up and talking to me. Whatever it was, it needed to be resolved before Sophie came home in a couple of days. I missed him already and I wanted nothing more than to wrap my arms around him and tell him that everything was going to be fine.

I spent the day running a couple of errands and then I took my guitar to Central Park and sat beneath the oak tree and played some music to soothe my soul. When I returned home, Oliver wasn't home yet and dinner was ready.

"He's not home yet?" I asked.

"No, but he called me and said that he won't be home until late tonight. I had already started to cook and I couldn't let it go to waste."

"Will you eat with me, Clara?" I asked with a sadness in my voice.

I wondered why he didn't bother to call and tell me. What was going on with him?

Clara fixed our plates and we sat at the kitchen table. "What's wrong, Delilah? Did something happen between you and Mr. Wyatt?"

I looked down as I swirled my fork around the mashed potatoes. "I don't know. When I woke up last night, he wasn't in bed. I went down to the living room and he was sitting at the piano with a drink in his hand. When I asked him what was wrong, he yelled at me and told me to go back to bed. He said he had a lot on his mind. But he wouldn't talk to me about it."

She sighed. "Mr. Wyatt is a complicated man. I've seen a lot of women walk in and out of his life over the past seven years. Elaine, Sophie's mother, was a troubled girl. I felt sorry for her. She was so in love with Oliver. I think it was more the lifestyle he could provide her and her obsession with him."

"How long were they together?" I asked.

"They really weren't together. They dated on and off for a few months. It was never anything steady. He never let anyone get close to him. He always kept the women he dated at a distance."

"Even Laurel?"

"Yes, even Laurel. I could never figure out what he saw in her to keep her around for as long as he did. I suspect it was because she was just like him and it was a relationship of convenience. But then again, I think she was starting to push him into getting closer and taking their relationship to the next level. Then you walked into his life." She smiled.

"Yay me."

"When he told me that he hired another nanny for Sophie, I rolled my eyes. I was giving it a week before she drove you out of here. When you walked through that door for the first time and I saw you, I knew right away you were the one."

"How?"

"I just knew, Delilah, and I think Oliver did too. He was different when he talked about you. I'm going to tell you something. All the women he's dated over the years, including Laurel, have never slept in his bed. You were the first and when I walked in that morning and saw both of your clothes lying on the kitchen floor, I was beyond happy."

"Really?" I smiled.

"Yes. You are changing him and I see it every day. He's more attentive with Sophie than he's ever been and he seems happier. That child also sees it and she loves you. The change in her behavior since you moved in is astounding."

"She just needed to feel loved and I could relate to that. I believe that was our connection."

Clara reached over and placed her hand on mine. "Don't worry about Mr. Wyatt. Whatever's bothering him, he'll come around and he'll talk to you. Don't give up on him yet. He has a lot of issues to work out."

"Thanks, Clara."

She got up from the table and took both our plates.

"You go home to your family. I'll clean this up."

"No. I'll help you." She gave a small smile.

We cleaned up the dishes and I gave her a hug goodbye. I went up to my room and looked at the clock. It read eight thirty. I sat down on my bed and strummed my guitar, working on some new melodies. Before I knew it, it was eleven o'clock and he still wasn't home. No phone call, no text message. Where was he? I got up from the bed and decided to go to the Red Room for a while and hang out with Jonah.

It was one-thirty in the morning when I walked through the door. I didn't know if he was home and I didn't care. I had a few White Russians and I was feeling it. When I reached the top of the stairs to the living room, I saw Oliver glaring at me from the leather chair.

"Where the hell were you?"

I held up my finger. "I was out. Where were you?"

"That's none of your concern. I'm your boss. You aren't mine."

Those words punched me right in the gut. He was looking for a fight and I had no idea why. "And it's none of your concern where I was either, boss. I'm not on the clock. Sophie isn't here."

"Don't you dare give me that attitude," he spoke sternly as he got up from the chair.

"I don't have the strength to argue with you. I need to go to bed."

"You've been drinking, haven't you?"

"Yes, I have and now I need to go sleep it off."

"You aren't going anywhere until I say you can go." He took hold of my arm.

I jerked away from him and stumbled from the dizziness I was feeling from the alcohol.

"What the hell is wrong with you?" I screamed. "Why can't you talk to me?"

He turned around and took a few steps away from me. "Just go to bed."

Now I was pissed off and I was going to get to the bottom of his sudden change. "No. I'm not going to bed until you tell me why you're acting like this."

"Go to bed, Delilah!" he yelled.

"I'm not going anywhere until you tell me why you're being such a dick!" My voice could have raised the dead.

He stood there and didn't say a word. His silence angered me. I walked up behind him and grabbed his arm.

"Damn you, Oliver. Talk to me! What the fuck did I do to deserve to be treated like this?" Tears had formed in my eyes.

He whipped his body around and grabbed hold of my arms, his face inches from mine. "You want to know what you did. You said last night that you loved me." He let go of my arms and turned his back on me.

"What? What are you talking about?"

"You were asleep and you said that you loved me. You broke my trust. You weren't supposed to fall in love with me."

The tears streamed down my face as I tried to comprehend his words. A sickness crept up inside of me and my heart ached. My chest tightened and I found it hard to breathe. I was falling apart, losing control, and there was nothing that I could do to stop it but give in and give up.

"You made me fall in love with you."

"Why? Because I fucked you? Is that all it takes for you to fall in love with someone?"

Cold hearted bastard. I couldn't respond. His words were like a knife through my heart. I walked away and went up to my room. I stripped out of my clothes and climbed into bed. I didn't have the energy to even put on my pajamas. I just wanted to crawl under the covers and die. I waited for him to come to my room and apologize, but he didn't. I thought I knew Oliver Wyatt. I thought I saw past his flaws and his pain, but I was wrong, and now, I had fallen in love for the first time in my life and it left me broken.

****

How was I going to face him after last night? I didn't even want to see him because the urge to slap him was still on the forefront of my mind. The only reason I slept was because of the alcohol I consumed. I looked at the clock as I rolled over, swollen eyes barely open. It was seven o'clock. If I stayed in my room another hour, he'd be gone to the office and I won't have to see him. I got up, took my time in the shower, got dressed, and looked at the clock again. It was eight fifteen. I walked down the stairs to the kitchen to find Clara cleaning up the breakfast dishes.

"Good morning, Delilah."

"Morning, Clara. Did he leave?"

"Yes. He's gone. What happened last night? He was in a foul mood this morning."

"He's not the only one." I poured a cup of coffee and took it outside on the patio.

As I was typing a text message to Liam, my phone rang with an unfamiliar number from Boston.

"Hello."

"Miss Graham?" the voice on the other end spoke.

"Yes."

"This is Massachusetts General Hospital calling. Your brother, Tanner, has been in an accident."

My heart stopped. "What? What kind of accident?"

"He was hit by a car. We feel you should get here as soon as possible."

I started to shake uncontrollably. "Is he alive?"

"Yes. But he's in very critical condition. It's imperative that you get here as soon as possible."

"Thank you. I'm on my way."

I went to get up from my seat and could barely stand. I gripped the arm of the chair for a moment to collect myself. *Okay, calm down. Gather your thoughts, Delilah.* The first thing I needed to do was book a flight to Boston. I called the airlines and asked when the next flight out was. Three hours. I booked the flight and went upstairs to pack my bag and grab my guitar.

"Clara, my brother was in an accident," I said with tears in my eyes.

"Oh no, Delilah. Is he okay?"

"He's in critical condition and I have to get there as soon as possible. I don't know when I'll be back, but I have to leave now."

"Do you need me to call Scott?"

"No. I'll take a cab."

"Take care of yourself, Delilah." She gave me a warm hug.

"Sophie is coming home tomorrow. Please keep an eye on her while I'm gone."

"Of course I will. Don't you worry about a thing."

I left the house, walked down the street, and took a cab to JKF airport. I sent a text message to Jenny.

"Tanner was in an accident and he's in critical condition at Massachusetts General Hospital. I'm on my way there now. I'll call you when I have more information."

"Oh my God. He'll be fine, Delilah. Do you want me to go with you?"

"No. Stay in New York. I'll be fine."

"Call me the minute you get to the hospital."

On my way to the airport, I pondered whether or not to tell Oliver. I had no choice; he was my boss and I wasn't going to be there when Sophie got home tomorrow. *Shit.* I was sure, after last night, I no longer had a job anyway. But, until he fired me, he was still my boss.

"My brother was in a bad accident and I had to leave to go be with him. I just wanted you to know that I don't know when I'll be back. Clara promised she would look after Sophie until I return."

I waited for a response and one didn't come through. I boarded the plane, turned off my phone, and curled up in my seat, praying to God that Tanner was okay.

Chapter 29

Oliver

I had been in meetings all day. Liam and I were about to head for a late lunch when I pulled my phone from my pocket and read Delilah's text message.

"FUCK!"

"What's wrong?" Liam asked.

"Delilah's brother was in a bad accident and she left to go be with him. Sophie's coming home tomorrow. She'll be devastated if Delilah isn't there."

"Seriously? Where did she go?"

"I don't know. She didn't say and the thing is, she has two brothers."

"Sorry, bro, but her brother takes precedent over you and Sophie."

"You don't think I know that?" I scowled.

"What's going on with you and her? You've been in a shit mood for the past few days."

"Nothing. I don't want to talk about it. Now let's go grab some lunch before the next meeting."

I wasn't ready to talk to Liam about what Delilah said because I knew if I did, he'd go into a long-winded speech, and I wasn't in the mood. I felt bad for what happened to her brother and wish I knew where she went off to. Maybe Clara knew. I dialed her.

"Hello, Mr. Wyatt."

"Clara, where did Delilah go?"

"I don't know. She didn't say."

"Did she tell you which brother was in an accident?"

"No. She just said she had to go and she packed a bag and left. Don't worry about Sophie. I'll take care of her when she returns tomorrow."

"Thank you, Clara. If you hear anything from Delilah, let me know."

I sighed.

"I was in meetings all day and just got your message. I'm sorry about your brother. Where are you?"

She didn't respond. "Text Delilah and ask her where she is. Maybe she'll respond to you," I said to Liam as we sat down for lunch.

"Why wouldn't she respond to you? What the fuck did you do to her?"

"Nothing. I'm not getting into this now. Just do it."

He sent her a text message and, as we ate lunch, he kept checking his phone. "She's not responding to me either. I swear to God, Oliver, if you hurt her in any way."

"Drop it, Liam. I didn't. We had an argument and I don't want to talk about it."

"Whatever. But I'm going to say this once and only once. If this has anything to do with what happened with Kristen, you better fucking get over it. Go seek therapy if you have to. Delilah is the best thing that has ever happened in your life, aside from Sophie, and you'd be a fool to let her go. Shit, if you weren't my brother, I'd go after her myself. It's been thirteen years, Oliver. Thirteen fucking years."

"Drop it!" I spat.

"I will for now because I said what I needed to say. Take my words and think about it."

We ate the rest of lunch in silence and then headed back to the office for another meeting.

****

Delilah

I went up to the ICU and the nurse took me to Tanner's room. I stopped in the doorway and stared at all the tubes and wires coming from him. His head was wrapped in white bandages, his face was bruised and swollen, and his leg was in a cast. Tears filled my eyes and I felt sick to my stomach as I began to shake.

"He's in a coma right now. I'll let the doctor know you're here and he'll be in shortly."

I placed my hand over my mouth as I walked over to his bedside and took a seat in the chair. The loud beeps of the machines brought me back to when my mom was in the hospital dying from liver failure. I couldn't lose Tanner. He had to be okay. I grabbed his hand and began to sob as I put my head down on the bed.

"Excuse me, Miss Graham?"

I looked up and saw a man in blue scrubs staring at me.

"Yes."

"Hi, I'm Dr. Noor." He extended his hand.

I unsteadily got up from the chair and lightly shook it.

"Tanner has sustained some pretty serious injuries. We had to go into his brain and stop some bleeding. We had to remove his spleen and his leg is broken in three places. He was barely alive when they brought him in. We did everything we could possibly do and now we have to wait and hope for the best. The next forty-eight hours are the most critical."

"What about his coma?"

"He slipped into that shortly after we stopped the bleeding in his brain. We don't know for sure how long he'll be in it. It could be hours, days, weeks, or even months. I'm so sorry."

"How did this happen?"

"We aren't sure. But there's a girl who's been in the waiting room since last night if you want to talk to her."

"Thank you, Dr. Noor."

"Have faith, Miss Graham."

I nodded as he gave me a small, sympathetic smile and walked out of the room. A moment after he left, the nurse walked in to take Tanner's vitals.

"Dr. Noor said there's a girl who's been in the waiting room since last night."

"Yes. Apparently, she's a friend of his and was there when the accident happened. If you'll give me a moment, I'll take you to her."

After she checked his vitals, I followed her to the waiting room. The distraught, brown-haired girl with the big brown eyes stood up and looked at me.

"Delilah?" she asked.

"Yes. I'm Delilah."

"I recognize you from the pictures Tanner showed me. I'm Addison." She started to cry.

I took her hand and we both sat down. "Can you tell me what happened?"

"We were coming back from a party and the car got a flat tire. Tanner pulled over on the side of the road. He told me to wait in the car. He was having trouble getting the tire off, so he stood up and tried to flag a car down for some help. Suddenly, out of nowhere, a car swerved and hit him."

"Did the car stop?"

"He stopped a few feet ahead and then took off. I could only get part of the license plate number. I told the police everything

I knew. Is he going to be okay? They won't tell me anything because I'm not family."

"I don't know if he'll be okay. He's in a coma right now."

"Oh God." She sobbed even harder.

"Why don't you go home and get some rest. Thank you for everything and for staying. You can come back later and I'll make sure the nurses let you in the room. I'm here now, so he's not alone."

"Okay. But I'll be back later."

"Are you his girlfriend?"

"Not yet. I had hoped to be."

I softly smiled at her as I gave her a hug. "He's going to be fine."

We walked out of the waiting room together and I went back to Tanner's room. I turned my phone on to call Braden and Colette. Several text messages came through from Oliver, Liam, and Jenny.

As I read Oliver's text, I felt twisted. I didn't respond to him because this wasn't his problem. I was sure he put Liam up to finding out where I was and I wasn't responding to him either. I waited until I composed myself before calling my other siblings. I needed to be strong, not only for their sake, but for

Tanner's as well. Braden was catching the first flight out and Colette broke down over the phone. She wouldn't be able to fly out for a few days because she was just finishing up her summer classes. She wanted to fly out today, but I told her that Braden was on his way and to stay put until her classes were over. I was angry, so angry that this had happened to him. He didn't deserve this. He was a great kid with a bright future. I took hold of his hand as I leaned over him.

"You will fight, Tanner Graham. Do you understand me? You will not leave us like Mom did. You're a fighter and now's the time you need to give everything you got to pull out of this. You've always listened to me and you're not going to stop listening now!" I sobbed.

Chapter 30

Oliver

Still no response from Delilah and I was pissed as hell. I blew it last night with what I said. I wanted to push her away because I wanted her to see that I wasn't a good man. I was far from it. She was such a kindhearted and selfless person and I didn't deserve her love. Fuck, I was in love with her and I was protecting her from me. I never gave Kristen the chance to tell me why she did what she did. I was so caught up in my own misery that I never even asked. I just yelled at her and broke it off without giving her a chance to explain. Did her explanation even matter? No, it didn't because she had hurt me in such a bad way that nothing she could have said would have made it better. Liam was right; it had been thirteen years. Thirteen years of closing myself off to another woman because of what she did. I loved Delilah and I wanted to keep her in my life. I wanted to make her mine and only mine. If I was going to make that happen, then I would have to do something I never thought I'd do and it frightened the fuck out of me. I pulled my phone from my pocket and sent Delilah another text message.

"I'm sorry for everything. Please let me know you're okay."

No response. I swallowed hard as I dialed her number and brought the phone up to my ear. It went straight to voicemail.

"Delilah, it's me. I've been texting you and you're not responding. I need to know that you're okay and I want to know how your brother is doing. I'm sorry for what I said the other night and we need to talk. Please call me."

The next morning, I woke up to the sound of the alarm. I reached over, shut it off, and grabbed my phone. Still no response from Delilah. I threw my phone across the bed and got up to shower. Walking downstairs, I found Liam standing in the kitchen talking to Clara.

"Have you heard from Delilah?" I asked my brother.

"No. She never responded to your text either?"

"No. Nor my calls or voice message. She has really gone and pissed me off. How am I supposed to know that she's okay?"

"Relax, Mr. Wyatt. She's fine. She's Delilah."

"You don't know that, Clara."

"What I do know is that maybe you shouldn't have yelled at her and made her feel bad. It's your fault she didn't tell you where she went. You have no one to blame but yourself. Now, excuse me. I have to prepare for Sophie's arrival."

"Oh snap." Liam smiled. "I guess she told you. What did you yell at her about?"

"I don't want to talk about it right now. Let's get to the office so I can get back home before Sophie arrives."

How was I going to tell Sophie that Delilah wasn't home? How was I going to tell my little girl that I didn't know where she was or when she was coming back?

****

Delilah

I held on to Tanner's hand as I rested my head on the edge of the bed.

"Sis."

I looked up. Braden was standing in the doorway. I got up and ran to him, hugging him tight. "I'm so happy you're here."

"How is he?" Braden asked as he slowly walked over to the bed.

"He's in bad shape." I held back the tears. I couldn't let Braden see me cry. I was the strong one to my brothers and sister. I was the glue that held the family together.

"He's going to pull through, right?"

"Yeah. He's going to pull through." I gave a small smile as I placed my hand on his cheek.

"Listen. My internship starts the day after tomorrow. So I'm going to have to leave in the morning. Unless you need me to stay."

"No. We'll be fine. He knows you're here now and that's all that matters. Tell me about this internship of yours."

"It's for one of the biggest finance companies in Chicago. Out of the whole program, they only choose two people to interview and I got the job. It's an internship for the summer and then in the fall, I'll work for them part time until I graduate and then, if I work out, they'll bring me on full-time."

"I'm so proud of you, Braden. Come here." I reached over and gave him a big hug.

"Thanks, Delilah, but I couldn't have done it without you. How are you? How's that nanny job going?"

"It's going good. Sophie is a wonderful and smart little girl."

I wasn't about to tell him about Oliver. There were things my siblings didn't need to know.

"Well, she's a lucky little girl to have you looking after her. Where are you staying?"

"Shit. Nowhere yet. I forgot to get a hotel room."

"What about Tanner's apartment?" Braden asked.

"Nah. He's only staying there for the summer and I don't know his roommate. That would be awkward."

"There's a hotel right down the street from the hospital. Why don't we go check it out and then bring some carryout back here?"

"Sounds good." I gave Tanner a kiss on his swollen cheek and told him that I'd be back soon. Braden and I walked down the street to the hotel and got a room for the night. I set my bag down but took my guitar with me. Tanner always loved it when I sang to him.

*****

Oliver

"Daddy!" Sophie squealed as she ran into my arms.

"Hi, baby. I'm so happy you're home." I spun her around. "I missed you."

"I missed you too. Where's Delilah?"

Shit. I thanked Matt and Kelsey for everything and they left. I took Sophie's bags upstairs and asked her to sit down next to me on her bed.

"Daddy, why isn't Delilah here?"

"Sweetheart. Delilah's brother was in a very bad accident and he's in the hospital. She had to go be with him for a while."

"Is he okay?"

"I'm not sure, princess. Delilah's been very busy taking care of him, so I really haven't spoken with her. But she told me to tell you that she loves you very much and she's sorry she couldn't be here, but she'll be home as soon as she can."

"But I wanted to see her now," she pouted.

"I know, but her brother needs her. You understand that, right?"

"Yeah." She looked down in disappointment.

"How about if we go out to dinner? Just me and you. Anywhere you want to go."

"Really?"

"Really."

"Okay, but I don't want to be gone too long because I want to paint."

I kissed her head. "I promise we won't be."

The two of us had a nice dinner and Sophie told me all about the farm and the animals. She seemed really happy and sending her to Vermont had been the right decision. After dinner, she painted for a while and then asked if I'd lie in bed with her and watch *Frozen*. Hell, I didn't even know what *Frozen* was, but I missed her and wanted to spend time with her. Halfway through the movie, she fell asleep. I turned it off, pulled the covers over her, and kissed her goodnight. After changing into my pajama bottoms, I picked up my phone. There were still no messages from Delilah. I hated the fact that I couldn't be there for her with what she was going through. I opened my laptop and started to do some work, but I couldn't concentrate. Shit, this was bad. I shut my laptop down and turned on the TV, something I very rarely did. I clicked on the movie section and searched for *The Notebook*. Once I found it, I hit play. In some ways, I felt closer to her, watching the movie she loved.

Chapter 31

Delilah

Braden and I left the hospital around eleven o'clock. We were both exhausted and I just craved climbing into a bed and going to sleep. I had seen earlier in the day that I had a voice message from Oliver, but I didn't listen to it. With Braden flying in and Tanner lying in the hospital bed, I just didn't have time. Or maybe it was because I couldn't bear to hear his voice. I washed my face, brushed my teeth, and by time I came out from the bathroom, Braden was already asleep. I pressed play and, instantly, my heart hurt when I heard his voice. He wanted to talk, but I couldn't deal with him right now. My main focus could only be my brother. He was worried and, even though he deserved to be punished for the things he said to me, I couldn't find it in my heart to let him worry.

"I'm okay."

Within seconds, his reply came through.

"Thank God. Can I call you?"

"No. I can't talk. Braden is sleeping in the bed next to me and I don't want to wake him. How's Sophie?"

"She's good. She misses you, but I explained to her why you had to leave and she understood. I took her to dinner and then she made me watch Frozen *with her."*

I smiled.

"It's her favorite movie. I'm happy you watched it with her. I have to go. I'm exhausted."

"Tell me where you are and I can be there in a flash. You shouldn't have to do this alone."

"I'm not alone. Braden is with me and Colette will be here in a few days. Take care, Oliver."

"Good night, Delilah. I miss you."

A tear fell from my eye when I read his last message. I missed him too and I needed him more than ever at this moment. I needed his arms around me, comforting me and telling me that everything would be okay, because that was what I'd done my whole life for everyone else and now, I just wanted someone to be there for me.

****

Oliver

Scott pulled up to the curb of the small jewelry store in Newark. The bells above the door rang as I opened it and stepped inside. Costume jewelry, purses, scarves, and other accessories lined the walls around the small space.

"Can I help you?" The brunette behind the counter asked.

I was nervous as hell. "Is Kristen here?"

"She's in the back. Let me go get her." She smiled.

I walked around, looking at the collection of necklaces and earrings.

"Hi there, how can I help—"

She stopped mid-sentence when I turned around and looked at her.

"Hello, Kristen."

"Oliver?"

I gave her a smile.

"Oh my God. It's been what, thirteen years? How are you?"

"I'm okay. How are you?"

"I'm good. I'm doing real well. Thanks. What are you doing here?"

She still looked the same, only a few years older. "I was hoping we could go somewhere and talk."

She gave me an odd look. "Is everything okay?"

"Yeah. I just need an answer to a question I've had for the last thirteen years."

"Let me grab my purse and we can go have coffee."

We walked down the street to the coffee shop and took a seat at a small, round table near the window. I gripped my coffee cup and swallowed hard in preparation of the conversation that was about to take place.

"So what did you want to ask me?"

"First of all, I want to apologize for the things I said to you that day before I left."

"There's no need to apologize, Oliver. I deserved it." She looked down and ran her finger around the rim of the coffee cup. "You had every right to say the things you did because what I did was wrong."

"Why did you do it, Kristen? That's the question I've had all these years."

"We had talked so much about our future and being together forever that it scared me. We were seventeen, Oliver. We were still in high school, having fun, partying, and breaking all the rules. We thought we were invincible. What seventeen-year-old doesn't think that? I wasn't feeling good that day and Jayce saw that I was home, so he came over and one thing led to another. There was a connection between us, something that I'd felt for a while but wasn't sure."

"Why didn't you ever tell me that? Why didn't you just break things off with me?"

"I didn't know how to. I was afraid to hurt you and I knew it was wrong. I felt guilty because I felt things with him that I didn't feel with you. I'm sorry, Oliver."

As I sat there and listened to her, I fully understood every word she said. That connection. The one that pulls you in so deep, you can't break it. The connection I had with Delilah was like nothing I'd ever had before, even with Kristen. It took me thirteen years to find that connection with someone.

"Was that the first time you slept with him?"

She nodded her head. "Yes. After you stormed out of my house and told me you never wanted to see me again, I wanted to run after you and tell you that you'd be okay and that one day you'd see that I wasn't the girl for you. You are okay, right?"

I gave her a small smile as I reached across the table and placed my hand on hers. "Yes, Kristen. I'm okay. You ended up marrying him, didn't you?"

"Yeah. We dated for a while, broke up, and then a year later, we got back together. We got married when I was twenty-two and we're still going strong. How about you? I don't see a ring on your finger."

"Nah. I never bothered with marriage because I hadn't found the right girl. I do have a daughter, though. She's five and her name is Sophie." I pulled a picture of her up on my phone and showed her.

"She's beautiful, Oliver. She looks a lot like you." She smiled.

"Thanks. Her mother passed away a while back and she's living with me full-time."

"So you're a single daddy."

"Yeah. It took some getting used to at first. How about you? Do you have any kids?"

"No. I'm not able to have any, so Jayce and I are looking into adopting."

"I'm sorry to hear that, but adoption is good. There are many children out there that need loving parents."

She gave me a small smile. "I better get back to the shop. I don't want to leave Holly there alone too long by herself."

We got up from our seats and walked back down to the jewelry store. "It was nice to see you again, Kristen."

"It was good to see you too, Oliver. I hope you find that special someone."

"I already have and she's amazing. Take care and good luck with the adoption."

"Thanks."

I climbed into the limo with a feeling of contentment. Now it was time to open my heart and tell Delilah how much I loved her. I just hoped she could find it within herself to forgive me and give us a chance.

****

As soon as I got back to the office, I called Liam to come in.

"What's up, bro?"

"Sit down. I need to talk to you."

"Sounds serious? Everything okay?"

"It will be, I hope. I went to Newark and had coffee with Kristen."

His mouth dropped. "What? Why did you do that?"

"I needed to know why she cheated on me."

"Did you get the answer you were looking for?"

I smiled. "Yes, I did, and it's time for me to move on. I'm going to fly to Boston to see Delilah and to make sure she's okay."

"How do you know she's in Boston?"

"We did a little bit of texting back and forth last night and she said she couldn't talk because her brother Braden was sleeping in the bed next to hers. She only has two brothers, so it would be Tanner that was in the accident and he's attending college in Boston. Now, I just need to find out which hospital he's at."

"They won't give out that information," Liam spoke.

"Then I guess I need to pay a visit to the one person who would know."

"Jenny?" he asked.

"Yep."

"I'll leave tomorrow morning. I also need you to hold down the company and, if you could, please spend some time with Sophie."

"No worries. Your daughter and our company is in good hands."

"Thanks, little brother. I owe you." I smiled.

Chapter 32

Delilah

Braden left yesterday morning to fly back to Chicago to start his internship. I spent the day at Tanner's bedside, talking to him and playing my guitar. His roommates and Addison stopped by to see him and sadness filled the room. There was a waiting room full of college students showing their support for him. I was touched, but not surprised. Tanner was always the popular kid and everyone loved him.

It was now day three. I walked into his room and opened the curtains so the sun could shine in.

"It's a beautiful day today, Tanner. I really would like for you to see it." I walked over to him and fluffed his pillow. "Braden starts his internship today and he's really excited about it, but he feels really bad that he had to leave. I told him not to worry about it because I was here to take care of you just like when you were younger. Colette called last night and her flight was cancelled due to some tropical storm that's brewing over

Florida right now. She'll be here as soon as she can get out and she sends her love. You should see the waiting room. It's filled with all of your college friends. They're being so supportive and want you to get better soon. I talked to the police yesterday and they're doing everything they can to track down the person who hit you."

I stood over him and ran my hand down his swollen cheek. "You will recover from this. You're not giving up because I won't allow it."

I grabbed my guitar and sat down in the chair next to his bed. "I stayed up last night and learned to play your favorite song. Let me know what you think." I began to strum and sing, "I Will Follow You into the Dark."

****

Oliver

I stood in the doorway of Tanner's room and watched the love of my life sing to her brother. The feeling that ripped through me was euphoric. I had missed her and seeing her again was like seeing her for the first time. Her voice, her heart, and her gentle soul radiated throughout the room. My insides twisted at the thought that she'd be pissed I was here. I didn't call. I didn't text. I just showed up because she needed me whether she believed she did or not. She had said she loved me and I knew she still did, or at least I hoped she did. This was no longer about lust. This was about love, something I deeply wanted with her. She finished her song and then got up and kissed her brother on the cheek. She looked over and an expression of shock swept over her face.

****

Delilah

"Oliver. What are you doing here?" I asked in shock, wondering if this was a dream.

He stepped inside the room. Walking over to me, he stopped within inches and stared into my eyes. "I'm here because you shouldn't have to face this alone." He ran his thumb down my cheek and, instantly, I began to cry. I buried my hands in my face so as not to embarrass myself, because when I saw him, everything that I had held back came rushing out. He wrapped his arms around me and held my head against his chest as I uncontrollably cried.

"It's okay, sweetheart. Let it all out. You don't have to do this alone anymore. I'm here and I'm not going anywhere." He pressed his lips against the top of my head.

The tears kept flowing and I couldn't stop them. It felt so good to be held by him. To feel safe and wanted. I couldn't think about the things he said. We'd discuss that later, after I finished my breakdown. Once my sobbing started to slow down, I apologized.

"I'm sorry." I wiped eyes.

"There's nothing to be sorry for." He reached over on the table, pulled a few tissues out of the box, and gently wiped the tears from my face.

After blowing my nose, I looked over at Tanner and then back at Oliver.

"This is my brother, Tanner."

"How's he doing?"

"He's stable now, but he's still in a coma. The doctors have no idea how long he'll be like this. But he's a fighter and he'll pull through."

"Of course he will."

"I can't believe you're here. What about Sophie?"

"Sophie is in good hands with Clara and Liam."

"And your business?"

"My business can wait. Right now, making sure you're okay is my top priority."

"But—"

He placed his finger on my lips. "No buts. Where's Braden?"

"He started his internship today back in Chicago. He flew out yesterday."

"And your sister?"

"She's stuck in Florida because of a tropical storm. All flights were cancelled. She'll be here as soon as she can get out."

"Then it's a good thing I'm here. Have you eaten?"

"No."

He pulled me into him. "Let's go down to the cafeteria and see what they have. The food on the plane wasn't very appetizing."

I let out a light laugh. "Believe me, the cafeteria isn't any better."

As we ate breakfast together, we talked about Tanner. I explained everything that happened the night of his accident. Then curiosity got the best of me.

"How did you know I was here? Wait, don't answer that. Jenny told you, didn't she?"

He took a bite of his bagel and smiled. "It took a lot of persuasion, but she finally told me."

"What kind of persuasion?" I asked with a sly smile.

"We can talk about that later. Where are you staying?"

"The Holiday Inn down the street."

He narrowed his eyes as he looked at me. "Really?"

"Yes, really. I can't afford high-end hotels, Mr. Wyatt. The Holiday Inn is just fine."

He chuckled. "Well, it's not for me. I'm a hotel snob and I have no shame in admitting it. Would you like to stay with me, in my suite, at the Fifteen Beacon, which is literally .5 miles down from the Holiday Inn?"

"A suite, you say?"

"Yes. A suite. A big suite that is too big for one person. It's the kind of suite that needs to be shared with someone special." He smiled.

"I'd like that." I bit my bottom lip and I could feel myself blush.

"I was hoping you'd say that." He reached across the table and took my hand, interlacing our fingers. "I missed you, Delilah."

"I missed you too."

As we got up from our seats, I grabbed the tray and Oliver took it from my hands and set it back down on the table. Smiling at me, he placed his hand softly on my cheek, then his lips gently brushed against mine. Heat coursed through my body and I smiled.

"People are staring."

"Who cares? Let them stare. I've missed those beautiful lips and I'm not waiting another second to kiss them."

After our small and passionate kiss, we went back to Tanner's room. As happy as I was that Oliver was here with me, I was confused by his sudden change. We spent the rest of the day by Tanner's bedside. I played my guitar while Oliver made some phone calls.

"Let me know when you're ready to go to the hotel," he spoke.

It was already eight o'clock and I was feeling drained. "I guess I'm ready now. It feels so much later."

Taking my hands in his, he interlaced our fingers. "That's because you're exhausted."

We walked out of the room and down to the Holiday Inn so I could grab my things and check out. When we walked into the room, I noticed Oliver looking around.

"It's not that bad." I laughed.

"No, actually, it's not."

He helped me gather my things and I shoved them in my suitcase. After doing one last check to make sure I hadn't forgotten anything, I checked out and we walked down to the Fifteen Beacon.

"Here we are." Oliver smiled as he opened the door.

I walked into the room and was blown away, not only by the size, but by the beauty of it.

"Wow. This is beautiful and it's certainly no Holiday Inn."

Oliver chuckled. "No. It isn't."

He set my suitcase down and I turned to him, wrapping my arms around his waist and laying my head against his chest. I wanted him. I needed him and my body craved him. He kissed the top of my head and held me tight.

"Delilah, we need to talk."

"I don't want to talk, Oliver."

He broke our embrace and placed his hands on each side of my face. "We can talk after I make love to you. But I want to say something first."

His eyes were locked on mine and I could see the passion in them.

"I love you, Delilah. I'm in love with you and I need you."

My lips formed a small smile and elation rushed through my body. "I love you too and I need you more than you'll ever know."

Chapter 33

Oliver

I let out a sigh of relief when I heard those words come from her. She still loved me and I was the happiest man on earth. To be loved by such a beautiful woman and soul was a gift from God, a gift that I wasn't sure I still deserved. My fingers gripped the bottom of her shirt and I carefully lifted it over her head. She stared at me intently as I unbuttoned my shirt and slid it off my shoulders. She placed her hand on my heart and smiled.

"You never had a heart of stone. It was just a little broken."

"And now, it's fully healed again because of you." I brushed my lips against hers and I reached around and unhooked her bra. My hands instantly latched onto her breasts as my tongue entered her mouth and met with hers. She took down my pants and ran her hand against my hard cock. I moaned with pleasure because it felt so good to be touched by her again. I needed to feel her and pleasure her. I wanted her to get lost in me and forget about everything else for a while. I unbuttoned her pants and slid them off her beautiful hips along with her panties so she was standing fully naked in front of me. She let out a soft moan as my tongue slid across the flesh of her neck and my hand made its way down. Dipping my fingers inside her and feeling how wet she was excited me even more. I turned her around and laid her face down on the bed, massaging her shoulders and back as my mouth explored every inch of her, right down to her perfect ass.

"That feels so good," she moaned.

"I want you to relax, Delilah. Let me take care of you."

After massaging her backside for a while, I turned her over and smashed my mouth against hers before traveling to her breasts and taking each hardened nipple in my mouth. I felt like I was about to explode and my cock hadn't even touched her yet. I spread her legs wide as I buried my head inside her thighs, flicking my tongue against her clit and dipping my fingers inside of her. Her back arched and her moans heightened. She was already about to come. Sucking her deeply and moving my fingers in and out of her sent her over the edge as her fingers tangled in my hair and she gave in to her orgasm. Her heart was racing and her skin was heated. I moved up and hovered over her, staring into her happy eyes.

"No more condoms. I fully trust you, Delilah. I want you to know that."

The corners of her mouth curved up as she pulled me down and passionately kissed me as my cock rested between her legs. Grabbing hold of it, I thrust inside her and we both gasped. Her legs wrapped around me as I buried my cock deep inside of her. I wanted to stay like this forever and I was never letting her go. I moved in and out of her at a rapid pace, enjoying her warmth and the pleasure she gave me. I sat up and held on to her hips as I moved in and out, watching the gratification on her face as I fucked her. My thumb pressed on her swollen clit as she was ready to climax again. Her body tightened as she threw back her head, calling out my name as she released herself to me. I closed my eyes as I felt the wetness rush like a wave over my cock. I pulled out and flipped her over. Spreading her legs and taking hold of her ass with my hands, I moved in and out of her and the pressure built and I was about to come. Her sexy moans and her telling me to go faster and harder sent me over the edge as I pushed as deeply as I could inside her with one last thrust and filled her insides with my come. The heat between us was undeniable and coming inside of her without a condom was the best feeling in the world. Once I finished, I lowered my head and my lips pressed against her back. When I collapsed on top of her, she reached her arm back and stroked my face with her hand.

I climbed off of her and pulled her into me. I didn't care about cleaning up; I just wanted to hold her in my arms.

"I love you," I whispered to her again. Words I never thought would be so easy to say were with her.

"I love you, Oliver."

We stayed wrapped up in each other for a few moments until I asked her if she would like to take a bath. I started the water and climbed in while she twisted her beautiful hair up with a clip. She climbed in and pressed her back against my chest as I wrapped my arms around her.

****

Delilah

Safety and comfort resided in me as I softly ran my finger around his arm.

"There's something I need to tell you," he spoke.

I looked up at him as his lips lightly touched mine. "What is it?"

"I had coffee with Kristen."

"Who?" I asked in confusion.

"The girl I dated back when I was seventeen. I guess I never mentioned her name to you. I'm telling you this because I don't ever want any secrets between us."

"Why did you see her?"

"I needed to put closure on what had happened and I needed some answers. Answers I never gave her the chance to give me back then."

"Did you get those answers?"

"Yes. I was already in love with you and I knew it. I just needed to put the past behind me."

"I'm happy and proud of you, Oliver."

His grip around me tightened. "You are the most special person in the world, Delilah Graham, and I've never felt this way about anyone before, not even her. I was young, stupid, and thought I was in love, but in reality, I wasn't and it wasn't until you walked into my life that I discovered that. You and Sophie are the most important people in my life and I'm never going to let either one of you go. So prepare yourself because you're mine forever."

"I like that idea." I smiled as I tilted my head back and he kissed me.

"Good, because it's time that someone takes care of you and that's what I intend to do. I will take care of you and make sure that your needs are fully met and fulfilled. I don't ever want to see you unhappy or sad."

His hard cock pressed firmly against my back. I turned around so I was facing him and sat up, pressing down until he was deep inside of me. His sexy lips curved into a smile.

"Wow. I didn't expect that," he moaned.

"Prepare yourself to always be surprised, Mr. Wyatt."

The next morning, as we were getting ready to go to the hospital, my phone rang and it was a face time call from Liam.

"Hi there." I smiled into the phone.

"Hey, good looking. How are you?"

"Hi, Delilah!" Sophie appeared with a big grin on her face.

"Hi, baby. How are you?"

"I'm okay. How's your brother?" she asked in her sweet voice.

"He's still in the hospital, but he's going to be okay."

"Good."

Oliver walked up behind me. "Good morning, princess."

"Hi, Daddy. Why are you in the same room with Delilah?"

"Umm. Well, I just came to get her because we're heading to the hospital now."

"Oh, okay. I just wanted to say hi. Uncle Liam is taking me to the museum today. I'm so excited!"

"That's wonderful, Sophie."

"Bye, Delilah. Bye, Daddy. I love you."

"We love you too, princess."

I heard Liam tell her to go get ready so they could leave. He took the phone from her hand and his face appeared on the screen.

"So, is everything okay with the two of you?" he asked with a wide grin. "Judging from the ripped apart bed behind you, I'd say things are really good."

Oliver rolled his eyes. "Yes, things are good. We'll talk later. By the way, if you're taking Sophie to the museum, who's taking care of the company?"

"The company is fine, Oliver. We're going to the museum and then Sophie's coming with me back to the office. Clara had some family thing to do today, so I'm spending the day with her. Don't worry about a thing."

"I'm not worried. Thank you, Liam, and have fun."

"Bye, Delilah." He smiled and kissed the screen.

I laughed.

"If you do that again to my girlfriend, little brother, I'll hurt you in more ways than one."

Liam laughed as he ended the call. I reached up and gave Oliver a kiss. "I like being your girlfriend." I smiled.

"Good, because I like being your boyfriend. Nothing gives me more pleasure. Well, except when I bury my cock deep inside that beautiful pussy of yours." He winked.

Instantly, I was aroused and aching for him. I wrapped my hand around the back of his neck. "We have about ten minutes. Show me how fast you can pleasure me."

He growled as he took down his pants and I took down mine. He pushed away everything that was sitting on the desk and lifted me up on it. "Have you ever had sex on a desk?"

"No." I bit down on my bottom lip.

"Good. Enjoy the ride, Miss Graham." His grin widened as he thrust into me.

Chapter 34

When we walked into Tanner's room, Oliver took a seat in the chair to check his emails and messages.

"Okay, Tanner. It's a beautiful day again today and I don't want you to miss it. You are to wake up and see the sun shining. Do you understand me?" I spoke harshly as I opened the curtains. I froze.

"Always telling me what to do," I heard his voice say in a whisper.

Oliver jumped up from his chair and I slowly turned around to see Tanner staring at me. "My head hurts, sis."

I ran over to him and began to cry. Oliver left the room to get the nurse.

"Oh my God, you're awake." I leaned over and lightly hugged him.

"It was your nagging voice." He tried to smile.

The nurse came running in and Oliver followed behind.

"Nice to see you awake, Mr. Graham," the nurse spoke as she took his vitals.

"Thanks. It's nice to be awake. My head hurts really bad and so does my leg."

"I'll get you some pain medication right now and I'll call the doctor."

Oliver walked up behind me and smiled at Tanner. "Glad you're okay, buddy."

"You must be Oliver," he whispered.

I looked at him strangely. "How did you know?"

"I just know." He stared across the room. "Hey, sis."

I looked over at the doorway and Colette and some guy walked in. I ran to her and gave her a hug. "He just woke up."

"Thank God." She let out a sigh of relief as she walked over to his bedside.

"Hi, you must be Delilah. I'm Corey. Colette's boyfriend."

"Nice to meet you, Corey. I didn't know Colette had a boyfriend." I looked over at her.

"I haven't had a chance to tell you yet."

"This is my boyfriend, Oliver Wyatt." I smiled with delight.

"I didn't know you had a boyfriend." She smirked. "Isn't he your boss?"

"Yes. Yes he is."

Oliver extended his hand to both of them.

"Hey. Can you all keep it down? My head is throbbing."

The nurse walked in and pushed some pain medication through his IV. "There you go. You should start to feel some relief any minute now." She smiled as she patted his arm.

****

A few days later, Tanner's condition was improving and Colette and Corey flew back to Florida. As our bodies were tangled in each other, Oliver kissed the side of my head.

"I need to talk to you about something."

"What is it?"

"I spoke with the doctor last night before we left and he said that Tanner is stable enough to be transferred to Mount Sinai Hospital in New York. Once his head injury is fully healed, we can bring him home with us and I'll make sure he gets the best possible care, including the best physical therapy for his leg."

"Oliver, I don't know what to say."

"Say yes and let's go home."

"I would love that, but we have to talk to Tanner first."

"I already did last night and he said he wants to go. The doctor said he can be transferred tomorrow."

I sat up and looked at him, the sheet dropping from my naked body. "Tomorrow? Really?"

His eyes raked over my body and fixated on my breasts. He brought his finger up to my nipple and softly traced around it.

"Umm. I'm sorry. What did you say? Oh yes. Tomorrow. We're going home tomorrow."

I laughed as I took the pillow and hit him with it. He sprang up and grabbed it from my hands. "I haven't had a good pillow fight since me and Liam were kids." He chuckled as he hit me with it. I grabbed his from underneath him and the two of us behaved like children, on our knees hitting each other with pillows, except we were completely naked.

"Stop," he commanded.

"What's wrong?"

"Watching your breasts bounce up and down like that is driving me insane." He grabbed the pillow from me and threw me on my back, hovering over me as he smashed his mouth to mine. "I need to fuck you right now."

"Stop talking," I commanded as my breath hitched between kisses.

****

Oliver

We took our seats in first class and Delilah looked around as she made herself comfortable in her seat.

"Is something wrong?"

"No. I'm just taking in the luxury of first class." She grinned.

"You've never flown first class before?"

Her grin disappeared as she shot me an "are you stupid" look. "No, Mr. Millionaire. I have never flown first class. Need I remind you where I came from?"

"Sorry." I took her hand and brought it up to my lips. "I happen to love where you came from." He winked.

"I'm so happy to be going home. I wish we could have flown in the helicopter with Tanner." A distressed look swept across her face.

"I know, but we'll arrive at the hospital just shortly after him. I think we need to talk about something."

"What?"

"We need to discuss our sleeping arrangements when we get home. I don't want Sophie—"

She placed her finger on my lips. "Don't worry about Sophie. We'll figure something out."

"I want you in my bed. I don't want to sleep alone ever again, but we need to be careful where she's concerned."

"Sophie is an extremely intelligent child. We're going to have to talk to her and tell her what's going on with us."

"I know and I don't know how," I expressed.

"We'll talk to her together." She laid her head on my shoulder.

Even though Delilah didn't seem too worried about Sophie, I couldn't help but be concerned about how she would feel. Delilah was right; Sophie was highly intelligent and that was what worried me.

The plane landed and Scott drove us to Mount Sinai, where Tanner was already situated in his room. We spoke to this attending doctor and I was going to make arrangements for a physical therapist to come to the house. I had a small room off the foyer that was unfurnished and never used for anything. I arranged for a decorator to come and turn it into a bedroom for Tanner since he couldn't walk up stairs. It would be perfect for him because everything he needed was on the first level. After spending some time with him, he ordered us to leave.

"You have to get home to Sophie. You've been by my side since the accident and I'm eternally grateful for that, but I'm not a child, Delilah. I'll be fine here. Just make sure you visit." He smiled.

She took his hand. "I feel bad for leaving you here."

"Don't be. Go home to that little girl. She needs you now. I have my cell phone right here. We can face time later."

We said our goodbyes and Delilah stepped out of the room. Before I walked out, Tanner called to me.

"Yeah." I turned around.

"Thank you, Oliver. Not only for what you're doing for me, but for what you've done for Delilah. She deserves to be happy."

"You're welcome and I love your sister very much."

****

As we walked up the steps, the front door flew open and Sophie came running outside.

"Delilah! Daddy!" She threw her arms around both of us.

"Hello, princess." I smiled as I kissed her head.

"Hi, my little ray of sunshine." Delilah bent down and swooped her up. "I missed you so much."

Liam was standing at the door, smiling at us as we walked inside.

"Hello, my favorite two people in the whole world."

"Bro." We hugged.

He leaned over and gave Delilah a kiss on the cheek. "I'm glad you're back. How's Tanner?"

"He's doing better. The doctor said he can probably come home in about a week."

"Good to hear."

Delilah put Sophie down as Clara walked into the foyer to greet us.

"Welcome home, Delilah and Mr. Wyatt." She smiled as she hugged us both.

It was good to be home. I took our bags up to my bedroom. Clara prepared a late dinner for us and, after we ate, Delilah and I took Sophie upstairs to have a talk with her. After Delilah helped her into her pajamas, the three of us sat on the bed.

"There's something we need to talk to you about, princess."

"Is it bad?" she asked.

I softly smiled as I pushed her hair behind her ear. "No, sweetheart. It's not bad."

"What is it, Daddy?"

I looked at Delilah and she nodded at me. "You know how you love Delilah?"

"Yes."

"Well, I love her too and the three of us are going to be spending a lot more time together and we want to know how you feel about that."

She looked at Delilah and then back at me. "Are you and Delilah boyfriend and girlfriend?" she asked with innocence.

"Yes, we are, princess."

"Does that mean you'll be sleeping in the same bed?"

I swallowed hard and looked at Delilah. She took Sophie's hands.

"Yes, Sophie. I will be moving my things into your daddy's room and I'll be sleeping in his bed."

I was mortified when she told her that.

"Okay." Sophie smiled.

I let out a sigh of relief. We tucked her into bed, kissed her goodnight, and walked out of the room.

"See, no big deal." Delilah smiled.

"I guess, but I'm not sure that I'm comfortable with her knowing that you'll be sleeping in my bed."

"That's not the only thing that I'll be doing in there." She winked.

My cock twitched and I grabbed her, picked her up, and carried her to our room. I threw her on the bed and hovered over her.

"I want you to show me what exactly you'll be doing in here." I leaned down and kissed her sexy lips.

Chapter 35

Delilah

A couple of weeks had passed and Tanner was settled into his new room and the house. Oliver had hired a homecare nurse to attend to him and monitor his progress. It was good having him here with us and Sophie really liked him. Now that he was settled, it was time to focus on Sophie.

The alarm went off and Oliver moaned. I opened my eyes and smiled as I stroked his muscular chest.

"What's the moan for?" I asked as I reached over and shut it off.

"The sound of that alarm is annoying. I'm still tired." He kissed my head.

"You should be full of energy after what we did last night."

"That's exactly the reason why I'm tired." He smiled.

"Don't forget that the psychologist is coming over today around noon to meet Sophie. Will you be able to be here?" My lips pressed against his chest.

"Yes. I'll be here."

I smiled as I kissed his lips and went into the bathroom. We showered, got dressed, and when I went into Sophie's room, she wasn't in there. I walked down to the kitchen and poured a cup of coffee.

"Good morning, Clara. Where's Sophie?"

"Good morning, Delilah. She went to Tanner's room."

"Ugh. I hope she didn't wake him."

I took my coffee and walked to Tanner's room. I stood in the doorway and found Sophie sitting next to him. She was reading to him.

"Good morning. You didn't wake Tanner up, did you, Soph?"

"No. He was already awake when I came in here."

"Why don't you go get ready for breakfast and I'll bring Tanner out."

"Okay." She smiled as she climbed off the bed and walked out of the room.

"She's a great kid, Delilah. I can't believe how smart she is. She was reading me a book about Van Gough. That's not normal for a five-year-old."

I laughed. "I believe Sophie is a little genius. We have a psychologist coming to the house today to evaluate her."

"Damn. I wish I was that smart."

"If she's bothering you, I can have a talk with her," I said as I helped him into his wheelchair.

"Nah. She's not bothering me at all. I like the company. Sometimes I feel like I'm talking to an adult." He chuckled.

"That's the problem. She can relate better to adults than she can to other children."

"If she's so smart, maybe she needs to be with other children that are on her level. She may find that ordinary kids are boring."

I gave him a perplexed look. "I hadn't thought of that. That's a good point."

****

"Hi, I'm Dr. Pettifeur."

"Come in, Dr. Pettifeur. I'm Delilah Graham."

"You can call me Elizabeth. I hate formality."

She wasn't anything that I expected. She was dressed in a pair of khakis, a white cotton button-down shirt, and a pair of loafers. Her blonde hair was pulled back in a high ponytail and she wore black-rimmed glasses. She looked to be about mid-thirties. I kept staring at her and she picked up on it because she asked if something was wrong.

"I apologize. I'm so embarrassed. I just thought—"

"Let me guess. You were expecting someone to look more professional? Sort of stuffy and uptight looking?" She smiled.

I had no words. She knew exactly what I was thinking.

"It's okay." She laughed. "I get that a lot. Being a child psychologist, I don't like to intimidate the children. It helps to be more on their level. I don't want them to think of me as a doctor because, frankly, doctors scare kids. I want them to think of me as their friend."

"That is so true. Again, I apologize."

"No worries." She gave a warm and friendly smile.

"Her father should be home any minute. If you'll follow me upstairs, I can introduce you to Sophie."

"All right, let's do this. It says in my notes that you're her nanny?"

"Yes."

Just as we were walking up the stairs, the front door opened and Oliver walked in.

"Oliver, this is Dr. Pettifeur."

"Nice to meet you." He held out his hand. "I'm Oliver Wyatt, Sophie's father."

"Nice to meet you, Mr. Wyatt. You can call me Elizabeth."

We continued up the stairs and to Sophie's room. When I opened the door, she was sitting down on her stool painting and, immediately, Elizabeth introduced herself before I could speak.

"Hi, Sophie, I'm Elizabeth. What a beautiful painting."

"Thank you."

Tears sprang to my eyes when I saw what she was painting. Oliver took note of my reaction and put his arm around me.

"If you don't mind, I would like to talk to Sophie alone. When we're finished, I'll speak to both of you." She gave us a confused look as she saw Oliver's arm around me.

We walked out of the room. "Are you okay?" he asked. "I noticed your reaction when you saw Sophie's painting."

"It's of my mom in Heaven. I had given her a picture of her last week. It looks like the same picture she painted of Elaine but with my mom."

He pulled me closer to him as we walked downstairs. "Did you tell Dr. Pettifeur, or Elizabeth, about Sophie's behavior at the play group last week?"

"No. Not yet. I haven't had the chance."

"Well, hopefully, we'll get some answers soon. I really didn't expect her to look like that."

"Like what?" I knew he was already thinking the same thing I did.

"So casual. She seems really nice and friendly."

"She seems very nice. She came highly recommended by Sophie's doctor."

"Don't you think it's odd that she introduced herself to Sophie as Elizabeth instead of Dr.?"

"She told me she doesn't like formality."

His eyebrow arched in that sexy way that made me want to kiss him passionately. "Oh. Okay, I guess sometimes formality isn't always a good thing."

I couldn't help but laugh. "How is work going so far?"

"It's fine. Liam seems out of sorts today. I'm going to have to talk to him to find out what's going on."

"Hmm. Girl problems?"

"I don't know. As far as I know, he's not seeing anyone. I'm going to go into my study and do some work. Come get me when she's finished with Sophie." His lips brushed against mine.

"I will." I smiled as I ran my thumb across his lips.

He leaned over and whispered in my ear. "You just made my cock twitch."

"Good." I winked as I walked away and went to the kitchen to talk to Clara.

A couple of hours had passed and Elizabeth came downstairs.

"All set?" I asked with a smile.

"Yes."

"Oliver is in his study. We can talk up there."

Nervousness settled inside of me as we walked into Oliver's study. He stood up and asked Elizabeth to take a seat while I shut the door.

"How did it go?" Oliver asked her.

"Sophie is an extremely intelligent child. She possesses an incredible artistic ability that most people could never have in their lifetime. I do believe your daughter has an extremely high

I.Q. level, but she'll need to undergo some extensive testing in order for us to be sure. She told me a lot about her mother, who passed away recently. She also talked a lot about you, Delilah."

"Oh?"

"Are the two of you seeing each other?" she asked as she looked at Oliver.

"Yes, we are. Is that a problem?"

"No. Sophie sees Delilah as the motherly type, which is good, don't get me wrong. But the attachment is so strong that if something should happen between the two of you, the effect on Sophie could be detrimental. Especially with her just losing her mother. Were you the only nanny Sophie has had since she came to live here?" she asked me.

"No." I looked at Oliver.

"There were about six others prior to Delilah. With Sophie's behavioral problems, they quit after a couple of weeks."

"I see." She wrote on her notepad. "Sophie told me that you sing, play the piano and the guitar."

"Yes. I do."

"That's how we met Delilah in the first place. We were at the diner she worked at having lunch and Sophie went into a meltdown after she had knocked over my cup of coffee. Delilah sat down next to her and started singing to her and, instantly, they connected. I had seen something in my daughter with Delilah that I hadn't seen before."

"Makes sense." She nodded her head. "Sophie connected with you because of your artistic ability. She considers you on the same level as her. Unfortunately for children of Sophie's status, they gravitate towards people who are equally as smart as them. Does Sophie have issues with other children?"

"Yes. I took her to a play group last week and at first she was fine, but as she was trying to play with the other children, she became agitated and shut down, yelling at them to go away and leave her alone."

"The problem with gifted children is that they often feel misunderstood and then they feel rejected, which in turn causes behavioral problems. She told me that you understood her need for reading and art and took her to the library and museum."

"Yes. I felt that in Sophie's situation, she needed to express herself, or cope, in an artistic way. For me, it's my music and I saw Sophie's artistic abilities in her drawings."

She gave me a smile. "You're very intelligent. No wonder Sophie connected with you so quickly."

"Thank you. But in reality, I'm not that smart."

"I think you are." Oliver winked.

"Okay. So here are my suggestions to both of you. Bring Sophie into my office and we'll test her and see how smart she really is. I pretty much already know her level, but we need a number for our records. Even though Sophie has the mind of an adult, she is a child and needs to be treated as such. Strict discipline is the key when appropriate. She also needs to understand that not every child is like her and that it's okay. This is the time where you need to push social interaction. She needs to learn that she fits into this world. She needs to develop a sense of belonging and, with the right guidance, which I do believe you both can give her, she'll gain that. I assume that she'll be starting kindergarten in the fall?" she asked with a twisted face.

"Yes. She'll be attending a private school."

"Okay. My suggestion to you would be to enroll her into a school for gifted children. If you throw her in a regular school, even a private one, she'll become bored and you'll have other issues with her. Her brain is like a sponge and it's absorbing all kinds of knowledge at an enormous rate. She needs to be in a program where she won't be bored and with others who understand her needs. It's very important. She won't be able to thrive in a classroom with ordinary children."

"We will certainly look into that," Oliver spoke.

"One last thing. I believe I have already gained Sophie's trust and I would like to see her once a month for a couple of hours to monitor her progress and behavior, if that's okay with you?"

"That sounds good. We can do that."

"Good." She smiled as she got up from her seat. "Parenting a gifted child isn't easy. You'll have ups and downs, but if you handle each situation correctly, she'll thrive into an amazing adult. Who knows? She may even change the world."

Oliver and I got up and shook her hand. "Thank you, Elizabeth."

"You're welcome. Also, gifted children are wonderful manipulators and I can guarantee that Sophie will, if she hasn't already, try to manipulate you. Don't let it happen."

Chapter 36

Oliver

I sighed as we walked Elizabeth to the door. I turned and looked at Delilah as I shook my head.

"What's wrong?"

"My head is spinning from all that information."

She laughed as she wrapped her arms around me. "She'll be fine. Who knows? Maybe by the time she's sixteen, she'll be a doctor."

"This doesn't bother you?"

"Why would it? Sophie is a normal child who has an exceptional brain. As long as we do the right things by her, she'll do great."

"I knew there was a reason I loved you other than the fact that you're a goddess in bed." He kissed my lips.

"I'm going to take that as a compliment, Mr. Wyatt."

"As you should, Miss Graham." I looked at my watch. "I need to get back to the office for a while. Why don't you tell Clara to take the rest of the day off and we'll take Sophie and Tanner out to dinner tonight. I think he would love to get out of this house."

"Sounds good. They'll love it."

I gave Delilah one last kiss and headed to the office. As I sat at my desk trying to concentrate on getting some work done, Liam walked in.

"Here are the contracts for the apartment building over on West 75th Street."

I could still tell something was off with him. "Sit down," I commanded.

"Okay. What's up?" He leaned back in his chair.

"What's going on with you?"

"What do you mean?"

"You can't fool me, little brother. I know something's bothering you."

He sighed as he laced his fingers behind his head. "I don't know, to be honest. I guess I'm feeling a little lonely."

I narrowed my eyes. "What do you mean?"

"Do I have to spell it out, Oliver? I want to meet the right girl."

"You date woman all the time. They practically fall at your feet."

"True. But none of them are the right girl and I know damn well you know what I mean."

I scratched the back of my head as I leaned back in my chair. "I do know what you mean and you will meet her eventually."

"I look at you and Delilah and I will admit that I'm jealous. She's an amazing woman and she's perfect for you. I want what you have. These relationships I get into are meaningless. I have yet to find that special woman who makes my heart skip a beat when she looks at me."

I took in a deep breath. I could feel my brother's pain and I didn't like it. "I know, and trust me, you'll find her when you least expect it. I'm a prime example of that."

"Yeah. It's weird how things work out sometimes."

"Listen, you're a great guy and a successful businessman. She's out there somewhere. Just be patient and one day, she'll pop into your life and you won't know what hit you. Until then, just keep having that meaningless sex." I gave him a wink.

"Thanks, bro."

"I'm taking Delilah, Tanner, and Sophie out to dinner tonight. Why don't you join us?"

"Nah. I have plans with Adam tonight. There's a bar calling our names."

I rolled my eyes. "Okay. If you change your mind, let me know."

"Thanks, Oliver. I'll talk to you later." He walked out of the office.

I felt sorry for him. He wasn't like me. He didn't put up a wall and he had no issues like I once did. He deserved to be happy and seeing him down and out like that killed me.

****

Delilah

Oliver took us out for a nice dinner and then after, we went to Central Park. It was a beautiful summer night and the park was alive with people and music. Oliver pushed Tanner in his wheelchair and I held on to Sophie's hand as we enjoyed the scenery and took in the different music that played all around. When we arrived back home, I helped Tanner into bed and Oliver took care of Sophie.

"Thanks for everything, sis," Tanner spoke as I helped him into bed.

"You're welcome. I'm just really sorry that you're going through this."

"I'm okay. I wouldn't have come this far without you."

I leaned over and kissed his forehead. "You're a lot stronger than you give yourself credit for."

"Thanks to you."

"Good night, Tanner. I'll see you in the morning."

"Good night, sis. I love you."

"I love you too." I blew him a kiss before leaving his room.

I walked upstairs and gave Sophie a kiss goodnight. When I walked into our bedroom, Oliver was undressing. A feeling of excitement overtook me as he slid off his shirt. His muscled biceps, well-defined six-pack, and strong, muscular back sent my panties into a soak fest. It didn't matter how many times I saw him without his shirt on, the same feeling revved throughout my body.

"I called The Anderson School today over on the Upper West Side and talked to them about enrolling Sophie in the fall."

"What did they say?" I asked as I took off my sundress and went into the bathroom to wash my face.

"They said that all applications had to be turned in last fall for this coming fall."

"Shit. Are you serious?"

"Don't worry, it was nothing that a little donation to the school couldn't fix." He walked up behind me and grabbed his toothbrush.

"A little donation? You mean you bought your daughter's way into the school."

"It depends on how you look at it. Sophie will be going there next week for testing. As long as she passes, she's in."

"So how much of a donation did you give?" I asked as I dried my face with a towel.

"A million dollars."

"A million dollars?!" I exclaimed. "Oliver."

He rinsed his mouth and I handed him the towel. "What? There's no price too great when it comes to the well-being of my daughter or my girlfriend."

"Is that so?" I ran my finger down center of his chest.

"It's very so." His lips seductively touched mine and his hands roamed up and down my sides. "Have I told you how fucking beautiful you are?"

"Yes. But feel free to say it again." I gasped as his tongue slid down the front of my throat and his hands unclasped my bra.

"You're so fucking beautiful." He pulled down my panties and lifted me up on the sink.

My hand traveled to the front of him, stroking his hard cock through the fabric of his underwear. He moaned and leaned down, taking in each of my breasts, licking and kissing until his lips wrapped around my nipple, sending me into a frenzy. His hand cupped me below before he dipped his fingers inside, feeling his way around and hitting all the right spots. I arched my back as he pulled his fingers out and brought me to the very edge, burying his head between my legs. His tongue circled my clit before engulfing my entire wet area with his magical mouth. The buildup was happening as I placed my feet on his shoulders and threw my head back, tightening my legs as the climax rushed through my body.

"Mhmm. That's what I like, baby." He stood up and smashed his mouth against mine for a passionate kiss before thrusting himself inside me. Sexual moans escaped both our lips as he moved in and out of me at a rapid pace, slipping his hands underneath me until my ass was held firmly by his grip. Another orgasm was coming as I swelled around his cock.

"You feel so good, Delilah. I never want to stop fucking you," he panted as he thrust in and out.

"I never want you to stop." My fingers dug into his flesh as he pounded into me with two last strokes sending my body into madness as we both released at the same time and him saying my name slowly as he poured every last drop of his pleasure inside of me.

I wrapped my arms around his neck as our lips passionately kissed and he held my face in his hands.

"I'm never letting you go," he whispered as he stared into my eyes.

"I'm never leaving." My finger ran down his cheek.

Chapter 37

Oliver

One Month Later

Everything was falling into place. Tanner was on his way to a full recovery with his leg and his physical therapy was going well. Sophie had tested almost perfect and was going to be attending first grade in the fall. She was going to be six years old and they said that because of her test scores, she should start in the first grade. Delilah's birthday was coming up and I had a plan to make it one she'd never forget.

It was a Saturday and I had arranged for Jenny to spend the day with Delilah. They needed a girls' day out. I booked them an all-day spa appointment, complete with massages, facials, manicures, pedicures, and body wraps. Plus, it was a way to get her out of the house so I could spend some time with Sophie alone. I brought her outside on the patio with me so we could have a little talk.

"What do you want to talk about, Daddy?" she asked as she dug into the bowl of ice cream I gave her.

"You know much I love Delilah, right?"

"Yes. I love her too."

"I know you do. I want nothing more than to spend the rest of my life with her and I want to ask her to marry me. How would you feel about that?"

Her eyes widened. "If you got married, then she would be my mommy."

"That's right, princess." I smiled. "I love her very much and I want us to be a family."

She set down her spoon and wrapped her little arms around my neck, giving me a big squeeze. "I want you to marry Delilah, Daddy."

"There's nothing I want more in this world, baby. Finish up your ice cream because I need your help picking out a very special ring for her, but you can't tell her. This is our very own little secret."

"I won't tell her. I promise."

"Good girl." I hugged her.

We went to Tiffany's and looked at all the engagement rings they had. There was one in particular that caught my eye. It was a two-carat, princess cut with beaded diamonds encased along the band. I picked it up and knew instantly how beautiful this would look sitting on her long, slender finger.

"That's one of our finest diamonds priced at $40,500.00," Frederick spoke.

"Sophie, what do you think about this one?" I held it up to her.

"It's so beautiful and sparkly. I think Delilah will love it." She smiled brightly.

"Me too. I'll take it, Frederick. Remember, Sophie, not a word of this to Delilah. We don't want to spoil the surprise."

"No worries. I won't tell her."

I kissed her head, paid for the ring, and then headed to the bookstore to buy Sophie some books. When we arrived back home, Delilah was in the kitchen making some tea.

"There you two are. Where were you?" she asked as I walked over and gave her a kiss.

Sophie held up her bag. "We went to the bookstore and bought some books."

"Awesome, Soph."

"I'm going up to my room to read them."

"How was your spa day?" I gripped her hips.

"It was amazing. Thank you again for doing that for us." She wrapped her arms around my neck and pressed her lips against mine.

"You're welcome. I hope you didn't make any plans for your birthday."

She gave me a strange look. "No. Not yet."

"Good, because I'm taking you to dinner in Fiji."

She laughed. "Okay, when do we leave?" she asked jokingly.

"We leave in three days," I spoke with seriousness.

Her smile left her lips as she stared at me. "You're serious, aren't you?"

"Yes. I'm taking you to Fiji for your birthday."

"Oh my God, Oliver. But what about Tanner and Sophie?"

"They're coming and so are Clara, Liam, and also Jenny and Stephen will be accompanying us."

She placed her hands over her mouth in shock. "Jenny knows about this?"

I smiled. "Yes, she knows. Everyone knows and they're excited to go. I hope you are too."

"Excited isn't the word, Oliver." She jumped up and wrapped her legs around my waist, kissing me a thousand times over. Nothing made me happier than to see the happiness and excitement that radiated throughout her.

****

Delilah

Oliver rented a private plane to fly all of us to Fiji. He didn't give me much notice and I had to spend the whole day before shopping for the appropriate vacation clothes. After a very long flight and then a short helicopter ride, we arrived at the Likuliku Lagoon Resort. I'd never seen anything more beautiful or spectacular in my life. Oliver rented all of us our own beachfront bures. Clara and Sophie had their own. Stephen and Jenny had theirs, while Liam and Tanner shared one. I was in awe of this place and the beauty it held. We all resided in our rooms for a while so everyone could get some rest after the long flight. Instead of resting, Oliver and I made love, ate chocolate-dipped strawberries, and sipped champagne. After having an extraordinary dinner, everyone was still jet lagged, so we called it a night. Even Oliver and I found ourselves completely drained, so we climbed into the king-sized luxurious bed and wrapped our bodies around each other as we drifted off into dreamland.

I awoke to the feeling of tiny kisses along my torso. I opened my eyes and smiled.

"Good morning."

"Happy birthday, sweetheart."

"Thank you and what a wonderful way to wake up."

"I'm giving you twenty-four beautiful birthday kisses." He smiled up at me as he took down my panties and spread my legs open.

His tongue, teasing me as he licked up my inner thighs and into my folds, lightly touching me and driving me insane with anticipation. The more he teased me, the wetter I became and he knew it. His tongue stroked my outer lips, circling back down to my thighs, creating such an intensity I thought I was going to burst.

"Please, Oliver. Please," I begged as my fingers tangled in his hair.

"Patience, sweetheart," he whispered as he dipped his finger slightly inside me.

I moaned and arched my back, begging for him to go deeper.

"Do you like it when I tease you like this?"

"Yes, but I need your mouth wrapped around me."

"It will be. Just a few more strokes and when my tongue sucks that beautiful clit of yours, you'll be having one of the best orgasms you've ever had in your life."

He had me flowing with excitement and he moaned as I soaked his fingers. He pulled them out and finally wrapped his mouth around me, sucking and licking my clit as it swelled with delight and my toes curled as my body climaxed. He didn't stop until I was finished and couldn't take it anymore. My heart raced and I was left breathless. He climbed on top of me and pushed himself deep inside me as he took my hardened and excited nipple in his mouth, sucking and licking like a wild beast. Each long stroke provided both of us with intense pleasure. He sat up and pushed my knees up to my chest, while he thrust in and out of me, causing me to swell around his cock as we both came in sync. I threw my head back and felt him explode inside of me as he moaned seductively and called out my name.

"God, I love you so much," he spoke with bated breath as he let go of my legs and collapsed on top of me.

I brought my hands up and held his head. "I love you more."

"Impossible." I felt his smile against my neck.

We got up to dress and then went to meet the rest of the gang and for breakfast. Oliver told me he had a surprise for me.

"What is it?"

"You'll see when we get to breakfast." He grabbed my hand and we went to the dining area of the hotel. When I walked in, everyone was already seated, waiting for us. My eyes locked on to Braden and Colette, who were sitting there with wide grins across their faces. Tears sprang to my eyes as I placed my hand over my mouth and they got up and walked over to me, hugging me tight.

"Happy birthday, sis," they both said.

"Oh my God. I can't believe you're here!"

"I wouldn't have them miss your birthday," Oliver said as he kissed the side of my head.

I turned to him and wrapped my arms around his waist. "Thank you so much. This is the best birthday I've ever had."

We spent the rest of day on the beach, talking, laughing, and drinking amazing cocktails. Sophie was having a wonderful time as she sat in the sand while she, Oliver, and Liam built sand castles. This was the best present Oliver could have given me and I was on top of the world. As I was getting ready for dinner, Oliver told me he was going to take Sophie down to the beach and to meet them down there when I was finished. After twisting up my hair and dabbing on some lip-gloss, I grabbed my sandals and carried them down to where Oliver and Sophie were standing a few feet from the water.

"Are you ready to go eat?" I asked as I approached them.

Oliver looked at me with a smile as Sophie took a step back. He took hold of my hands and took in a deep breath.

"Delilah, from the first moment I laid eyes on you, I was captivated by your beauty. Not only by your looks, but by your warm soul and kind heart. You are what dreams are made of. You're the light in my day and the stars in my night. You're the warmth when I'm cold and you're the air that I breathe. You are my entire world and I will love no other like I love you. You are in my soul and in my heart forever. We started as friends, and then as lovers, and now I would love if you'd do me the honor of becoming Mrs. Oliver Wyatt and be mine forever."

Tears sprang to my eyes as he reached into his pocket, got down on one knee, and slipped a ring on my finger.

"Will you marry me, Delilah? Will you be mine and Sophie's forever?"

"Yes! Oh my God, Oliver, yes. I will marry you!"

"Yay!" Sophie squealed.

Oliver stood up and kissed me. As we hugged, Sophie wrapped her arms around our legs and squeezed tight. I looked at Oliver and smiled as he bent down and picked her up.

"She said yes, princess."

"I know, Daddy. I heard."

I couldn't help but laugh as I took her from his arms and hugged her. This moment was so surreal and I never wanted it to end. I set Sophie down and took her hand as Oliver hooked his arm around me and we walked to the hotel for dinner. As we entered the dining room, Oliver yelled, "She said yes!" All of our family and friends clapped as they walked over and congratulated us.

"Welcome to the family, sis." Liam smiled as he gave me a hug and kiss.

We spent the rest of the evening celebrating with fine food, birthday cake, and wine. Clara took Sophie back to the room after dinner while we all stayed and celebrated, not only my birthday, but our engagement into the wee hours of the night.

Chapter 38

I returned to New York with a stunning ring on my finger and a sexy and beautiful man as my fiancé. A few days later, we flew with Tanner back to his apartment in Boston to help him get settled. He was doing much better and ready to get on with his schooling and life. He still needed some more therapy, but he was getting stronger every day. Oliver had made all the arrangements at a physical therapy facility that was right by the university. Addison was waiting for us at his apartment and was ecstatic when she saw him. I didn't have to worry because she promised to take care of him and he welcomed it.

The night we returned to New York, Oliver was sitting in bed with his laptop as I had just walked in after checking on Sophie.

"She's sound asleep. I think tomorrow I'm going to take her shopping for some school clothes."

He looked up at me from his computer. "Sounds like a good idea. Maybe you can swing by the office and we can grab some lunch."

"We can do that. Sophie will love it." I pulled my shirt over my head and tossed it in the laundry basket in the closet.

"Stop right there," Oliver commanded.

"What?"

"I want you to slowly take down your pants." He smiled.

I unbuttoned them and shimmied them off my hips, slowly and seductively as the hunger in his eyes grew. I stood there in only my lace bra and matching thong.

"Turn around so I can see that beautiful ass of yours."

I did as he asked and he let out a growl. "Now take your bra off and then turn around and face me."

I unhooked my bra, slowly and seductively taking down one strap at a time while I turned my head and smiled at him.

"Fuck." He took in a sharp breath.

I tossed my bra on the floor as I covered my breasts with my hands and slowly turned around. He closed his laptop and set it on the floor as his eyes raked over my body.

"Let me see those luscious breasts and slowly take off those panties."

I hooked my fingers into the sides of my thong and took them down as I moved my hips back and forth. I could see his hard-on poking through the sheets from across the room.

"Perfect. Now come here."

I walked over to his side of the bed as his hands latched onto my breasts, tugging at my already hardened nipples. His hand moved down south as he ran his fingers along my slick and aching spot.

"You're already wet and I've barely touched you. Do you know how much that turns me on? Climb up here. I need to taste that sweetness."

I bit down on my bottom lip as I straddled him and lowered myself down on his face. His tongue moved around me in circles and then softly stroked me up and down as I moved my hips back and forth across him. His hands reached up and kneaded my breasts as I swelled and fell over the edge into the pure bliss of yet another amazing orgasm. He moaned as he lapped up the wetness that spilled from me.

"That's what I like, baby. Now sit on my cock and take me inside of you."

I slid down and lowered myself on his rock hard cock, placing my hands on his chest and feeling his heart rapidly beat. He moaned in excitement as he threw his head back when I took him fully inside of me. His hands gripped tightly on my hips as I moved back and forth.

"I want to get married on Sweetest Day."

"Next year?" I asked with bated breath.

"No. This year. I don't want to wait to marry you."

"But that's in less than two months. There's no way." I continued to ride him.

"It can be done and we'll have a lot of help. I want you to be Mrs. Oliver Wyatt as soon as possible. Oh God," he moaned as I circled my hips. "Say yes."

"Yes. Yes. Yes," I wailed as another orgasm ripped through my body.

Before I knew it, I was on my back and he was thrusting in and out of me at a rapid pace.

"Yes to October, or yes because you just came all over my cock?"

"Both." I smiled.

His thrusting became wild. He was an animal out of control and I loved it. Heat tore through me as he halted, pushing as deep as he could inside me.

"Thank you," he spoke with bated breath as he filled me up with his come. He reached down and kissed my lips before collapsing on top of me, our heart rates out of control.

"Thank you for saying yes to the date or for your orgasm?"

"Both." He smiled as his lips pressed firmly against my neck.

****

Oliver

"You nervous, bro?" Liam asked as he straightened his bowtie.

"Nah."

"Bullshit. I can tell. You're literally shaking." He laughed.

"I am not. Okay. I'll admit I'm a little nervous."

"Don't be." He patted my shoulder. "You and Delilah are an amazing couple and she's so in love with you. You're lucky, bro."

I looked at him with a small smile. "You'll be here someday, Liam. Don't give up."

"I'm not and I know the right girl is out there somewhere. I just need to find her. Now let's get to Central Park so you can marry the love of your life."

I gathered up the rest of my groomsmen, a couple of friends of mine, Braden, and Tanner, and took the limo to the Conservatory Gardens. Our wedding planner, Bianca, made sure that everything was perfect. She had worked her ass off on such short notice, but she pulled it off and was generously compensated for her work.

I stood in front of the beautiful magnolia-laced archway and stared out into the crowd of people that had gathered to celebrate our marriage. The music had started and it was time. Nerves settled inside of me as I waited for my bride to walk down the aisle.

"You ready? This is it." Liam smiled as he placed his hand on my shoulder.

I took in a deep breath. "As ready as I'll ever be."

The bridesmaids walked down the aisle with the groomsmen and took their places in front of the arch. A smile graced my face when I saw my daughter walking down in her beautiful white dress as she threw red rose petals on the ground. She walked up to me and I bent down and gave her a kiss before she took her place on the other side. The bridal march had begun to play and my heart began to rapidly beat. I lost my breath as I saw Delilah walk down the aisle towards me with a beautiful smile on her face. She had never looked so stunning as she did at that moment. She was a queen, a goddess, and she was mine forever.

She approached me and I reached out and took her hand. "You look so beautiful," I whispered.

"So do you." A tear formed in her eye.

The ceremony began with the minster saying a few words and then it was time to say our vows. Liam handed me the ring as I took Delilah's hand and placed the ring on her finger.

"This ring is a symbol of my love and eternity together. You have made me the happiest man alive and I promise to take care of you and fulfill your every need for the rest of my life. I will take care of you in sickness and in health. I will be your rock when you need me to be and I will spend my life loving you. With this ring, I thee wed."

Jenny handed her my ring as she took my hand and slipped it on my finger. She stared deeply into my eyes as she said her vows.

"This ring is a symbol of my love and our eternity together. I can't imagine marrying a more perfect man. Your heart is a heart of gold and I will love you for the rest of my life. I give to you my life, my soul, and my heart. I will take care of you in sickness and in health and I will stand by your side forever. With this ring, I thee wed." A single tear fell down her cheek.

"I now pronounce you husband and wife. You may kiss your bride," the minister spoke.

I took my thumb and gently wiped away her tear as I pressed my lips against hers for our first kiss as husband and wife.

"I give to you Mr. and Mrs. Oliver Wyatt."

Everyone stood up from their seats as clapping and whistling was heard throughout the park.

"I love you." I smiled.

"I love you." She smiled back as we kissed one more time.

After taking what seemed like a million pictures, Delilah, Sophie, and I climbed into the back of the limo and headed to The Plaza Hotel for our wedding reception.

Chapter 39

Delilah

The reception was perfect. About six hundred people gathered to help celebrate our marriage. The ballroom was exquisite and elegantly decorated with beautiful flowers and white linens with silver overlays. The crystal chandeliers that hung from the ceilings displayed a low lighting, giving the atmosphere of pure romance. Oliver and I walked around and greeted our guests, thanking them for coming out to celebrate with us. After eating an elegant five-course meal, it was time to give my husband a surprise. I took my place on the stage as Jonah sat down at the piano and began to play the music I wrote.

"I wrote this song for you, Oliver, and I hope you like it."

I began to sing "Loving You Forever" as he stood in the center of the dance floor and watched me, our eyes never leaving each other and a smile across his face.

Once my song was over, I stepped off the stage as the band began to play our wedding song, "Unforgettable," by Nat King Cole. Oliver held out his hand as I took it and we shared our first dance as husband and wife. All eyes were on us.

"That song was beautiful. I will never forget it." He smiled at me and brushed his lips against mine.

"Thank you. I meant every word of it. I love you so much, Oliver. Thank you for walking into my diner and sitting in my section."

He chuckled. "It was fate, sweetheart. I was meant to find you, make you mine, and love you for the rest of my life."

We shared another long kiss as the guests clapped and shouted. We spent the rest of the evening celebrating our marriage and having a wild time. Liam was the life of the party when he took Sophie on the dance floor. Jonah and I showed off some of our musical talent together and we laughed and drank until Oliver whisked me away to the honeymoon suite and we made love for the first time as Mr. and Mrs. Oliver Wyatt.

****

Life was wonderful. We spent a week in Aruba, enjoying each other and soaking up the sun. When we got back home, life returned to normal. Oliver continued making his company a success and I still performed my music occasionally at the Red Room. Sophie liked her school and was doing very well in her classes. There were times when she still had her moments, but overall, she was an amazing kid. The first time she called me "Mom" at the wedding melted my heart and brought me to tears. My brothers and sister were thriving in college and moving on with their lives, while Liam was still on the prowl, in search for the perfect woman that would sweep him off his feet. It's amazing how your life can change in the blink of an eye. One minute I was a waitress in a greasy diner, and the next, I was a wife to the most incredible and sexy man on the face of the earth and a mother to a beautiful and highly intelligent little girl. I was nothing but a girl from the wrong side of the tracks of Chicago with a dream. A dream that one man alone fulfilled. I was Mrs. Oliver Wyatt and I was the happiest woman alive.

About The Author

Sandi Lynn is a New York Times, USA Today and Wall Street Journal bestselling author who spends all of her days writing. She published her first novel, Forever Black, in February 2013 and hasn't stopped writing since. Her addictions are shopping, romance novels, coffee, chocolate, margaritas, and giving readers an escape to another world.

Please come connect with her at:

www.facebook.com/Sandi.Lynn.Author

www.twitter.com/SandilynnWriter

www.authorsandilynn.com

www.pinterest.com/sandilynnWriter

www.instagram.com/sandilynnauthor

https://www.goodreads.com/author/show/6089757.Sandi_Lynn

Playlist

This Far ~ Kina Grannis

Jackson ~ Johnny Cash & June Carter Cash

Cups ~ Anna Kendrick

Let Her Go ~ Jasmine Thompson

Nothing Without Love ~ Nate Ruess

Love Today ~ Mika

Over You ~ Ingrid Michaelson, A Great Big World

Angels ~ Joshua Radin

Midnight Train To Georgia ~ Gladys Knight & The Pips

Never Let Me Go ~ Florence + The Machine

I Will Follow You Into The Dark ~ Jasmine Thompson

Halo ~ Beyonce

Unforgettable ~ Nat King Cole

Printed in Great Britain
by Amazon.co.uk, Ltd.,
Marston Gate.